SCOUT'S LAW

HENRY VOGEL

Published in the United States of America by Rampant Loon Press, an imprint of Rampant Loon Media LLC, P.O. Box 111, Lake Elmo, Minnesota 55042. "Rampant Loon Press" and the Rampant Loon colophon are trademarks of Rampant Loon Media LLC.

www.rampantloonmedia.com

Cover art by Jeff Doten.

ISBN: 978-1-938834-72-1 (ebook)

ISBN: 978-1-938834-73-8 (print)

First publication: November 2016

For the gang from the Friday Challenge. None of the Scout books would exist without your support and encouragement.

BLOOD AND SILENCE

Person Unknown

Silence. At long last, silence.

The inspection visit by Prince Rupor and his moronic galactic bride, Princess Heidi, threw the entire camp into an uproar. I knew they were coming. Everyone on the team did. I expected *some* disruption to our routine. I did not expect ten citizens of the Terran Federation to react like starstruck teenagers at the prospect of meeting one of the most famous couples in the galaxy.

My companion and I found our teammates' behavior appalling, fawning as they did over this so-called prince from one of the most advanced nations on Aashla. The planet is one of the most barbaric and least advanced human-settled planets in the galaxy. Worse, our camp was the last stop on our backward guests' extended inspection tour of scientific expeditions on Aashla. Prince Rupor's insatiable appetite for new scientific and engineering knowledge—which means virtually everything known to mankind—played right into our teammates' desperation to impress the barbarian prince. Equipment was unpacked and shown off without regard to procedure. Components we desperately needed were left in untidy and unsorted piles as learned men and women dug out favorite scientific instruments and showed them off to the royal couple.

And I couldn't walk more than five meters without tripping over one of their damned Tartegian royal guards. Unlike their prince, the guards were unimpressed with the scientists and their toys, and far too observant. When my companion and I didn't fall all over ourselves to impress their charges, we drew their unwelcome attention. I was forced to play the introverted researcher who was too shy to speak to the prince and princess. Once the royal couple 'drew me out,' I feigned the same enthusiasm as the rest. The effort was exhausting, but the guards turned their attention elsewhere.

After three interminable days, the inspection ended. The Tartegians boarded their airships and flew away. My companion and I coaxed and goaded and bullied the rest of the team into putting the equipment back in order. Even then, our teammates prattled on about our departed guests. And when they had wrung that subject dry, they immediately turned their attention to the next inspection and their chance to meet another pair of famous royal twits—David Rice and Princess Callan. The inane chatter tried my patience in the extreme, but it did leave our ten teammates in a celebratory mood.

My suggestion that we open some of the wine Prince Rupor gave us was met with enthusiasm. I took charge of that task, making it incredibly easy for me to drug the wine. Within an hour, our teammates were fast asleep in their bunks. My companion balked at the final task, but I expected that. Sending him off to begin digging, I took care of the researchers.

One by one, they awoke after the slash of my knife. One by one, they stared into my eyes with terrified incomprehension. One by one, I smiled and stroked their heads as the light faded from their eyes. One by one, I ended their prattle.

Finally, there was only silence. At long last, silence.

And then it was time to begin our *real* work.

A FOND FAREWELL

Jade

Mom had me cleaning the toilet when Forbose arrived. Dad brought the new device back from his last trade trip to Mordan and Mom was really proud of our indoor facility. God knows, I didn't miss the privy—especially on cold days—but Mom was nuts about keeping the new equipment clean. I suppose I could see her point since everyone who dropped by made an excuse to use it. And knowing some of those people as well as I did, they would certainly pass judgment on us based solely on how clean the crapper was.

Anyway, I heard the knock at the door and hoped it was Forbose. Maybe he could free me from this drudgery.

Mom answered the door and I could hear the tinge of disapproval in her voice. "Hello, Forbose. What can I do for you?"

Forbose either didn't pick up on Mom's tone or ignored it. "Good morning, Mrs. Cochran, and may I say you are looking lovely this morning?"

"You may."

That was one of Mom's irritating little tricks—giving answers to obviously rhetorical questions. Silence stretched and I could imagine Forbose trying to figure out why Mom was just looking at him. I really like Forbose—maybe even more than like him—but he's not good at subtleties.

Letting a little of my own disapproval tinge my voice, I shouted, "Mom is waiting for you to tell her she's looking lovely, Forbose!"

Another few seconds passed, then Forbose said, "You're looking lovely this morning, Mrs. Cochran."

"Why, thank you, Forbose. That's very kind of you to say. We're rather busy this morning, so if there's nothing else, I'll let you go about your day."

I heard the creak as Mom began shutting the door and rolled my eyes. It was going to be one of *those* days.

Forbose was quicker on the uptake this time. "Um, I was hoping to get a chance to say goodbye to Jade before I report to my airship tomorrow morning. It's my first run as a hand on the *Sorrin* and I'll be gone for three weeks."

Silence fell again as Mom considered the request. We really weren't that busy and I was close to finishing with the toilet. I knew Mom was weighing her disapproval of Forbose against dealing with a sulky sixteen-year-old daughter all day. Since Forbose was leaving soon, Mom knew I'd be extra sulky. I crossed my fingers and hoped that would tip the scales in my favor.

"Jade," Mom called, "Forbose is here to see you."

Ha! Score one for the teenager.

I scampered for my room, calling, "I'll be right there. I'm just going to put on some clean clothes."

I threw the bedroom door shut, startling my little sister Sasha from playing with her dolls. We shared the room, so she was getting used to me doing this. Sasha watched as I pulled off my shirt and pants and looked in my closet for something to wear.

"What's going on?" Sasha asked.

I held up a clean blouse and pair of pants. "Do these go together?"

Sasha may only be six, but she already has a better fashion eye than I'll ever have. She considered my choices for a few seconds and then shook her head. "Wear the red blouse. It goes better with your green eyes."

Pulling on the clothes, I muttered, "My clothes are supposed to match my eyes?"

"And your hair," Sasha said, "but blonde goes with almost everything."

"Oh my gosh, my hair!" I finished wriggling into the clothes and grabbed the hand mirror. I yanked off the scarf holding my hair out of my way and dragged a brush through it a few times. "How do I look?"

Sasha gazed at me in consideration for a few seconds. "Tuck in the blouse and you'll look better than Forbose deserves."

What was it with my family and my sort-of-boyfriend? I stuck my tongue out at her.

Sasha grinned and, in a sing-song voice, asked, "Are you going to kiss him?"

That was a good question. Was I going to kiss Forbose? Yes. Definitely. But what if he stuck his tongue in my mouth? I'd heard about that from some of the other girls. It sounded gross, but they said they liked it. Would I do the tongue thing? Maybe. We would see. But he was leaving for three weeks, so...probably.

I dashed back out of the room. Over my shoulder, I called, "Thanks, Sasha!"

Mom and Forbose were still standing at the doorway. Mom looked happy just standing there, blocking the door. Forbose looked relieved to see me.

I stopped and gave Mom a quick kiss on the cheek. I always reward good parental behavior in the hopes it will encourage more of it. "Thanks, Mom!"

Before I could skip past her, Mom caught me in a quick hug. She took that opportunity to whisper, "Don't let him pressure you into doing something you don't want to do."

I resisted the urge to heave a dramatic sigh or roll my eyes. It would just irritate Mom and she might even revoke her permission to go out. I slipped from her arms with a non-committal nod. I took Forbose's hand and we walked down the street.

We talked a little about his coming trip, which Forbose saw as his final step from boyhood to manhood. If Dad was here, he would insist it was just the first step. But Dad was still off on a trading run and wouldn't be back for another couple of weeks. At least, that was one bit of disapproval I dodged. I tried talking about how Dad was taking the whole family on the next trade run to show I had something in common in Forbose. He just sort of grunted in response and turned the talk back to his trip and everything he was sure he would do.

"I almost hope some raiders take a crack at us so the *Sorrin* can show those bastards a thing or two." I knew this was just boasting on his part. Nobody with any brains hopes for a raider attack. But Forbose didn't act like he knew that. "I've been practicing swordsmanship with some of the other guys who have signed on with airships. We're getting real good, too."

About then, I noticed Forbose was slowly steering us toward the lake. That's where those girls went when they learned about the tongue thing. Some of them learned a lot more than the tongue thing, too. I wondered how long it would be until one of them found herself having a hasty wedding. Still, I *had* decided to let Forbose kiss me and the lake was the place for that.

We made our way along the path, passing a few secluded spots already occupied by other couples. From the sounds, some of those couples were doing a lot more than just kissing. By the time Forbose found a spot for us, my heart was hammering in my chest. He led me through the bushes, pulling down a colored cloth laid across one bush.

"I came down here earlier and marked a spot for us," he said. "I didn't want to have to drag a blanket and stuff with me—especially with the way your Mom is."

I felt an irrational urge to defend Mom, but swallowed it. "What stuff did you bring?"

We pushed through one last bush and into a small clearing. The trees and bushes muffled the sounds from the lake and the city, making it seem like we were all alone. A blanket was laid out on the ground, along with a small basket.

"Oh, a picnic!" I exclaimed, finding the idea very romantic. I imagined it was the kind of thing David Rice would do for Princess Callan, and that made it even better.

"Yeah, sort of," Forbose said. He dropped to the ground and held out his arms. "Come here, Jade."

Okay, that was not what I was expecting. At least, not this quickly. But maybe Forbose had something else going on today and there just wasn't as much time as I thought. I sat and leaned into his embrace. Suddenly, he pulled me around and shoved his lips against mine. I tried to pucker up and let my body melt against his, just like it happens in adventure books. Then I felt a tongue shoving its way between my lips. Without thinking, I closed my teeth. Instead of blocking the tongue, I bit it.

"Ouch!" Forbose yelped, pulled back. "Why the hell did you do that, Jade?"

I sat back, surprised and a little hurt at his tone. "I...I wasn't... You just surprised me, is all."

Forbose nodded and reached for the basket. "I'm sorry, honey. I should have known you'd need to relax a bit."

He pulled out a dark-colored bottle and popped out the cork. Tilting the bottle back, Forbose took a long drink from it. Then he handed it to me. "Take a swig of this. It'll help you get relaxed."

Taking the bottle, I felt the little thrill you get from doing something forbidden. I'd had wine before, of course, but always at home and with Mom and Dad. I wasn't allowed to drink it outside of the house, even if they were both with me. Grinning at my boldness, I turned the bottle up and took a big drink—and almost choked as the liquid burned down my throat.

Gasping and coughing, I wheezed, "That's not wine!"

"Nope. This is rum—a *man's* drink." Forbose took another long drink.

I shook my head when he held it out to me again. I already felt something from that first drink. Something warm and relaxing radiated from my stomach. This time, when Forbose kissed me, I didn't resist. This time, when I felt his tongue on my lips, I opened my mouth and let it in. His tongue shoved hard against mine and I thought I could see how this might feel good and intimate, but not the way Forbose was doing it.

He leaned into me, continuing his attack on my tongue. I felt him pull my blouse up. His hand snaked under the suddenly free tail of the blouse and caressed my side. And then his hand began working its way up and around to the front of my body. I knew what he was reaching for and, worse, I realized Forbose wanted more than I was ready to give him.

I pulled my head back and grabbed his hand. It took both of my hands to push his hand down, then I scrambled back. "No!"

Forbose looked surprised and even a little hurt. "What's the matter, baby? I thought you wanted to show me how much you love me."

Did I unconsciously send that signal? I must have, because I was sure Forbose would never hurt me. And he was just sitting there, looking at me with that hurt puppy-dog expression on his face. Finding my voice, I said, "I'm sorry, Forbose. I don't know what I did to make you think I was ready for that. Please don't hate me."

"I could never hate you," he said, scooting close to me.

He kissed me again, this time gently and without the attacking tongue. It was nice, so I didn't stop him when he slid his hand inside my blouse again. This time, it didn't stray any higher than my waist, so I let it stay there. We kissed like that for a few minutes and then Forbose broke it off.

"I almost forgot—I'm supposed to report to the *Sorrin* this afternoon. We'd better go."

I knew he was lying—he told Mom he had to report tomorrow morning—but I just nodded. "I'll help you fold the blanket."

"Don't bother. I'll just leave it in case someone else wants to use it."

He led me out through the bushes and back toward the city. Just before we reached crowded streets, I said, "I'm sorry I disappointed you, Forbose."

"It's okay, Jade. You just weren't ready, yet. But now that you understand my needs, I'm sure you'll be ready when I get back from this trip." He pulled me close and wrapped an arm around my waist. "I want your mind *and* your body to understand just how much I love you."

"I'll...think about it," I said. "And maybe I will be ready for that when you get back in three weeks."

But the *Sorrin* never returned, making it the third Oshwindon-flagged trader to disappear that month.

ENSIGN'S ORDERS

Chris

I know I'm supposed to be sad when ground leave ends. I'm supposed to get upset at the thought of leaving home, of not seeing my parents, brothers, and sisters for a month or more. Whoever decided I should be upset didn't live with my family.

Don't get me wrong, I love them dearly. But life as the youngest of seven children isn't easy. I grew up wearing hand-me-down clothes, all of them heavily modified by my mother because the three children closest to my age are my sisters. I never had any privacy, either. And while I don't have any privacy as an ensign in the Navy, I have small areas of the ship that are mine and uniforms that weren't handed down. I also have responsibilities and even some modicum of respect.

So getting orders to report to the *Vanguard* the next morning was just fine with me—especially when I read our mission. It wasn't even a secret, so I could brag about it to my friends. And to Becca. And maybe she'd be impressed enough to walk with me and maybe, just maybe, give me a goodbye kiss.

I slipped out of the house, skirted past Dad's shop, and headed for the merchant docks. We always gathered there as kids, watching the big airships coming and going. Wondering where they were bound and what they carried in their holds. We still gathered there, even though most of us were seventeen. A couple of the gang were still sixteen, but none of us were younger than that.

I found the whole group gathered around someone who was sitting on the edge of the fountain and regaling them with some tale or the other. The guy had everyone's attention, that's for sure. Becca, especially, watched him with her eyes shining in a way they never did when she looked at me. Tony saw me coming and waved at me. The guy talking turned to see who Tony waved at.

"Sam!" I called. "When did you get in?"

Sam was eighteen and used to be the leader of our little group. He had signed on with a big merchant airship six months back and this was the first anyone had seen of him since. He flashed the big, infectious grin all the girls loved.

"Chris, lad!" Sam always lorded his superior age over us every chance he got. Obviously, six months aloft hadn't changed that. "They tell me the Navy took you on as an ensign."

"Aye, sir, that they did," I replied, puffing up just a bit. A commission in the Navy should be more impressive than a crewman's berth on a merchantman. If only I could convince my friends of that.

"They must be really hard up for good men if they took you, lad!" Sam delivered the line with a good-natured laugh, but its real purpose was to make sure I understood who was in charge.

"Ha, ha," I pasted on a smile to show I wasn't offended. "But, hey, I just got orders for my first real cruise—and wait until you hear what it is!"

"Is it fighting raiders?" Becca asked, her tone short.

"No, but it is—"

"Then shut up and sit down," she said, turning her shining eyes away from me. "Sam was just telling us about a raider attack on their ship."

"Really? Well, I'm all ears." I plopped down next to Tony, unable to get any closer than that to Becca.

Sam gave me a hard stare for a second and then returned to his story. I wondered what the stare meant, but I figured it out pretty quickly. Sam told an exciting story filled with swarming raider ships and fancy airship maneuvers. Of scrambling through the ship's lines as the raiders rained crossbow fire on his ship. And, of course, culminating in a harrowing battle to repel boarders.

I'll give Sam top marks as a storyteller. He had great timing and played up the gallantry of the rest of the crew, but he was certainly the hero of the piece. You could tell because he downplayed his part even while always managing to land right in the middle of the action every time. I was even pretty certain there was some small nugget of truth to the story—probably the bit about fleeing from raiders. But anyone with airship training—especially airship combat training—could tell he was making most of it up.

The stare was a warning not to ruin his moment. So I just listened and made all of the appropriate noises at all of the appropriate times. I didn't even say anything when, upon wrapping up the story, Sam and Becca walked off arm-in-arm.

"That was some story, huh, Chris?" Tony asked as I watched the pair walk away.

"What?" I looked back, belatedly catching Tony's question. "Yeah. It was quite a story."

"Well?" Tony asked.

"Well what?" I replied.

"You said something about orders. Are you going after raiders or something exciting like that?"

"Better! The *Vanguard* is part of the escort for Princess Callan's inspection of the galactic research stations."

The look of anticipation on Tony's face vanished completely. "Oh. Well, I'm sure you'll manage to learn all sorts of galactic stuff. And you're bound to get a chance to see Her Highness in person. I can see getting excited about *that*."

The others were already drifting away, obviously sharing Tony's opinion of my upcoming mission. I'm sure it will be a big moment to see our beautiful princess in person—not to mention our greatest hero, David Rice—but it wasn't like I would actually get a chance to talk to them or anything. Lowly ensigns don't get those opportunities. Just as lowly ensigns don't get the chance to fight shoulder-to-shoulder with the famous Captain Rice. And it's not like an inspection tour will require any fighting. I mean, who would be foolish enough to attack three Mordanian airships-of-the-line, not to mention an expedition led by David Rice?

No, I wasn't going to come back with stories to rival Sam's lies. And I obviously wasn't going to find Becca waiting anxiously for my safe return.

SUDDEN STORM

David

I awoke suddenly as something leapt upon me. As another weight landed on my stomach, I risked a glance at Callan. Through tousled raven hair, one green eye cracked open and surveyed the scene. With a groan, she pulled the covers up over her head.

"Daddy! Daddy! Wake up, Daddy!" Two bright green eyes peered at me through equally tousled raven hair from no more than six inches away.

"Don't be so loud, Anne!" Five-year-old Rob's head appeared next to my daughter's. "Mommy's sleeping."

Callan's arms snaked around Rob and pulled him into a hug. "Mommy *was* sleeping—until the two cutest raiders on Aashla woke her up."

Rob gave his mother a pained expression. "Anne is cute. Uncle Martin says I'm *dashing*."

Callan laughed. "Well, if Martin says it, it must be true. My apologies, dashing raider Rob."

Anne gave me a serious look. "Can I still be cute?"

I caught Anne's sides and lifted her above me. "You'll always be cute to me, honey."

"Is it time to go in the spaceship yet?" Rob asked, still snuggled against Callan.

"What time is it?" Callan asked.

"Almost six o'clock," Rob replied. "Aunt Sandra told us to let you sleep late this morning."

Anne held her arms out to me, so I brought her down into a hug. "Yeah, we've been waiting forever to come wake you up! And I'm hungry."

I sat up, throwing aside the covers on my side of the bed. "Well, why don't the two of you get dressed. I'll take you down for some breakfast and we'll let mommy get some beauty rest."

Anne crossed her arms and glared at me. "Mommy doesn't need sleep to be beautiful!"

I tapped the end of Anne's nose. "You're right, Little One. Sleep just helps her stay beautiful. Now come on you two."

Callan was up and dressed by the time the three of us came back from breakfast. She took over watching the children while I shaved and dressed for the day. We spent the next two hours making sure everything the kids would need or desperately want was packed. It was good we checked, too, since Anne's favorite stuffed tammar was still in her bed and Rob's treasured toy space-ship was under a pile of toy soldiers.

Eventually, Sandra and Harris—his first name is Terrance, but not even my sister uses it—showed up. The couple looked disgust-ingly well-rested.

Sandra cocked an eyebrow at the scene. "I told them to let you sleep late."

"Oh they did," Callan said, flashing an evil smile at the couple. "They didn't wake us up until nearly six."

"Don't worry, though," I added. "Once they get over the excite-ment of being on a spaceship with their aunt and uncle, I'm sure they'll let the two of you sleep even later than that!"

The next hour and a half passed quickly as we saw to loading the children's things onto the shuttle, gave them time to wish farewell to their grandparents—King Edwar and Queen Elaina to the rest of the kingdom—and then got in our own farewells.

"You two behave yourselves for Aunt Sandra and Uncle Harris, okay?" Callan said, hugging them in each in turn.

"And give Grandmama and Granddaddy Rice a big hug and a kiss from me," I added. "Your mother and I will come join you before you know it."

Arms around each other, Callan and I waved until the shuttle flew out of sight.

For the next two days, Callan and I tried to adjust to life without the children. It was easy at night, as we could relax in each other's embrace without worrying about a child's cry disturbing us. In the mornings, we found ourselves waking up at six o'clock even without energetic bundles leaping on us.

During daylight hours, we reviewed our plans for an inspection tour of Terran Federation facilities on Aashla. Inspections are an important of the oversight provision in our aid agreement with the Federation. Callan and I alternate tours with Rupor and Heidi, from neighboring Tarteg, so at least one person born in the Federation is present during every inspection.

Finally, we double-checked right of passage documents from every kingdom on our flight path. Satisfied everything was in order, I piloted our small airship into the bright blue sky above Morda. Three Mordanian warships—the real reason the rights of passage were so important—formed up around us and we set course for the first inspection site.

The next three weeks passed without incident. We inspected four sites and found encouraging signs of progress at each site. The fifth site on our tour was new to us. It was a desert research station and they'd been unpacking when Rupor and Heidi toured six months ago. So you can imagine our surprise when we reached its location and found nothing but a collection of abandoned prefabricated buildings.

Doors swung in the gentle breeze, creaking and scraping from the sand gumming up the hinges. We found nothing but drifting sand and dark brown splatters inside of the buildings. I thought the splatters were long-dried blood and sent for the ship's doctor.

Our careful search turned up no indication of what had happened to the station. Even the worst of disasters leave behind some kind of evidence and this one was no different. Three hours into our search, a shout arose from one of the naval parties.

Rushing to their location, we found the four airman gathered around a grisly sight. A desiccated hand jutted up from the ground.

A too-young ensign—he looked like he didn't need to shave more than once a month—swept an arm over the area around the exposed hand. "One of the men noticed the ground here wasn't packed as hard as you'd expect in a desert. He poked around with his sword and unearthed the hand"

"You have an alert crew," I said, squatting down and examining the hand. "Get a team out here with shovels and let's see who or what else is buried here."

Behind me, I heard a minor commotion as some of the airmen tried to stop Callan from joining me. "Not a fit sight for a lady" and similar other phrases floated my way. There was no doubt this crew had never traveled with my wife before.

"You're wasting your time, gentlemen," I called without looking up, "and we'll all live longer, happier lives if you accept the inevitable now."

A pair of small boots stepped into my peripheral vision. A lilting voice completely at odds with the scene before me asked, "You've sent for a team of diggers?"

"Yep. One thing I can't understand is why this grave was so hard to spot. In a desert like this, disturbed ground is usually visible for years."

"Couldn't wind speed the process?" Callan asked.

"Yes, but it would have to be a very strong wind—stronger than you normally find in this desert." I stood and looked around. Seeing nothing unexpected, I said, "Maybe a sandstorm swept through the area. Whatever it was, it doesn't matter now."

The Ensign returned and stood on the other side of me. I didn't look up but was certain I'd find a young man struggling to keep his eyes on the ground and off of Callan. "Trog attack, do you think, sir?"

I shook my head. "Trogs don't bury the dead. They'd either leave the bodies where they fell or, if the men fought well enough to earn their respect, the trogs would have cremated the remains."

"Perhaps a disease of some sort with the last survivor burying the dead?" mused the young man.

"You're over-thinking it, Ensign," Callan said in a matter-of-fact tone. "Chances are these men were killed by other men who buried the bodies to hide their actions for as long as possible."

"But who would want to kill innocent researchers?" the Ensign asked. "Desert tribesmen? Raiders?"

I stood and stepped back as men arrived with shovels. "Or a member of the research team."

"But they're *galactics*, sir!"

I exchanged a glance with Callan. Some people—especially young people—thought of galactic citizens as some form of an improved species of humanity.

"They're still just people, Ensign."

"People like *you*, sir."

Callan took my arm. "Also people like Caudill and the band of pirates who crashed here six years ago. And every kind of person in between those extremes."

The Ensign didn't appear ready to give up his cherished notion of galactic superiority but also chose not to argue with the heir to his country's throne and her transplanted-galactic husband. He covered his uncertainty by issuing mostly unnecessary instructions to the team of diggers.

Just as the men uncovered the first body, the expedition's surgeon, Dr. Mach, arrived. He spent the next fifteen minutes examining what was left of the first three bodies before speaking to Callan and me.

"I'll have to examine each of the bodies as they're uncovered, but these three people had their throats cut." He removed his spectacles and cleaned them absently. "Murdered in their sleep, I'd guess."

"What makes you say that, Doctor?" Callan asked.

"The wounds are too straight and clean. You only get that kind of wound if the victim isn't struggling." Putting his specs on again, Mach looked back at the mass grave. "How many people were on this research expedition?"

I checked the paperwork. "Eight men and four women."

"Why don't you and Her Highness find a comfortable place to wait? I'll bring my results to you once I'm done here." He glanced at the Ensign, pale-faced and swallowing hard at the sight taking shape before him. Lowering his voice, Mach added, "Perhaps you could find something to occupy young Marlow's mind, sir? I'm confident the men will find a way to finish digging without his instructions."

"I'll take care of the Ensign," Callan said, releasing my arm. "Don't let him drop me, darling."

Callan took two steps toward the Ensign then brought an arm to her forehead. "Oh dear, my head is spinning!"

Drawn by her voice, Marlow turned toward Callan—just in time to catch her as she gracefully tumbled into him.

"Your Highness!" the lad managed to exclaim before catching her. Eyes wide, Marlow turned imploring eyes toward the doctor and me.

Mach pretended to take Callan's pulse before using that most amazing medical procedure—the pat on the wrist. "I'm afraid the heat has affected Her Highness. Marlow, take the princess back to her airship. A little water and rest and she'll be just fine."

Marlow looked back and forth between Mach and me. "But shouldn't Captain Rice—"

"I have things to discuss with the good Captain before he can return. I know you would prefer to stay, Ensign, but your duty to our future queen outweighs your duty here." Mach gently turned Marlow to our ship. "Do stay with her until she releases you. There's a good lad."

Callan winked at us as she let Marlow lead her back to our ship.

Watching them go, Mach added, "He's a good lad and as smart as they come at that age, but I'm not sure he has the constitution for Navy life." Turning back to me, the doctor asked, "Shouldn't there be a lot of confusing equipment around here? Devices and widgets and all those other technical things these unfortunate souls needed to perform their research?"

"That's been uppermost in my mind ever since we landed, Doctor." I pointed toward the largest of prefabricated buildings. "Most of their equipment should have been in there, but it's empty."

"Did they have any galactic-style weapons? From what I've heard, I could readily see someone killing for those."

"No, Federation law expressly forbids bringing those to worlds such as Aashla. That wouldn't stop some people, but the previous inspection didn't find anything. Rupor and Heidi are thorough, so I doubt they overlooked anything." I pulled out the equipment manifest and read through it. "I suppose it's possible someone could make something dangerous out of all of this stuff. I'm not an engineer, though, so can only guess."

"What are your plans, Captain Rice?"

"I'll send one ship to the nearest Federation consulate to report this crime. The rest depends on what we dig up."

Two hours later we had our answer. We found the bodies of seven men and three women in the mass grave. As the sun sank beneath the horizon, the expedition's chaplain held a service for the dead. I tried to pay attention and show proper respect for the dead, but my mind kept returning to the one truly important question I had.

Were the missing man and woman responsible for the murders? If so, what plans did they have for the missing equipment and where did they go with it? Whatever covered the mass grave would have also wiped away any tracks left by the pair, but I didn't imagine they could go very far in this inhospitable land.

A somber mood lay over us as the officers gathered for dinner with Callan and me. Inspection escort duty was a popular assignment, with interesting sights to see and people from the stars to meet. Not to mention giving them a chance to travel and interact with the beautiful heir to their country's throne. Unfortunately, this trip wasn't following the traditional script.

"How do you wish to proceed, Your Highness?" Captain Jorson, the commander of the escort squadron, asked.

"We've got to get word to the Federation," Callan responded, "and try to find the two missing members of the scientific expedition."

Jorson grimaced. "Contacting the Federation would be a trivial matter if they would send us some of their communication devices. I can understand the ban on weapons, but—"

"There are excellent reasons for those prohibitions, Captain," Callan said. "Pardon me for interrupting, but imagine a band of raiders equipped with comms. Or the navy of one of Aashla's less savory rulers. The level of coordination such devices allow would go a long way to offsetting advantages in training and equipment."

Jorson reddened slightly, perhaps embarrassed that he had not thought of this angle or perhaps irritated that a young woman—even his future ruler—dared to lecture him on military matters. This was my first time working with Jorson and he'd shown himself a competent commander thus far, so I chose to give him the benefit of the doubt.

"I am just frustrated at the time it will take our messenger to reach the nearest Federation consulate, Your Highness."

"I share your frustration, Captain. That is why I want you to send a ship right after dinner. The sooner the message is away, the sooner it arrives."

Jorson flashed a brief smile and stood. "My thoughts exactly, Princess Callan. By your leave, I'll make the arrangements now."

Callan nodded. "David will record a message for your ship to carry."

I pulled a small message capsule—allowable technology as only someone with an implant could read from or record to the device —from a pocket and handed it to Jorson. "Already done, Captain. This has everything we know about the situation right now."

Callan looked around at her officers. "We'll gather back here once the ship is away. I'd like to begin our search tonight, if possible."

The senior officers nodded and returned to their own ships to prepare for the search. Within seconds, only Marlow—conveniently assigned as Callan's attendant in camp—remained with us. Lost in thought, the young man missed his cue to clear away Callan's dinner. At a nod from my wife, I gathered our plates while she watched the young man. Only when I took Marlow's plate did he break from his reverie with a start.

"Oh my goodness! My deepest apologies Your Highness!" He leapt up, reaching to take the plates from me. "I'll take those, Captain Rice."

Being quite capable of handling a little cleanup for myself, I was tempted to argue with the lad. I also knew the Ensign would face some form of discipline if his commanding officer learned the young man didn't do this himself.

As I handed the plates to Marlow, Callan asked, "What were you thinking about just now, Ensign?" A gentle smile lit her face. "Perhaps thoughts of a special young lady back home?"

The young man blushed. "No, Your Highness, there's no young lady waiting for me. Not yet, anyway. I was planning the most efficient search pattern for the local terrain."

I cocked an eyebrow at Marlow. "You were doing this planning without any charts?" Marlow nodded and my other eyebrow rose to join the first one. "Have you travelled this area before?"

"No sir." Marlow shook his head. "I just pictured the charts in my mind."

That's when Captain Jorson and his ship's officers rejoined us.

One of the escort ships rose into the darkening sky as the charts were spread on the table. I kept an eye on Marlow as the officers debated the best way to perform the search. The Ensign did a good job of hiding his opinion, but I saw he wasn't impressed with the plan. Callan saw it as well.

"Excuse me, gentlemen," she said, "but I'd like to hear what Ensign Marlow has to suggest."

Jorson and his officers jerked upright in surprise at Callan's suggestion. I caught just the hint of a smile on the lips of Captain Wright. I had no doubt Wright was Marlow's commanding officer and knew what was coming.

Marlow swallowed visibly under the glares of the gathered officers, but at Callan's nod he stepped between two stiff lieutenants and up to the table. He stammered when beginning his explanation but, once into the details, spoke with calm and conviction. A minute later, the skeptical officers were nodding at each point the Ensign presented.

"Well done, Ensign," Jorson said before looking at the gathered officers. "Are there any questions?"

When there weren't, the men reported to their ships. Jorson assigned three airmen to assist Callan and me. It would be our task to act as messengers between the two searching vessels. Minutes later, all three ships ascended. We waited, circling above the remains of the research station while the other ships split up and began their search.

Flying under the light of the planetary ring should have been quite romantic, but sharing the deck with three airmen rather ruined the ambience. It also made for a boring several hours as we waited for a signal from any of the searching ships. Finally, the ship to our southwest—the *Vanguard*—fired off a flare. Relieved to have something to do, I pointed our small ship southwest and off we flew.

I didn't notice the wind at first, attributing it to the simple fact that we were finally underway. Within a few minutes, it was obvious we were flying into an increasing headwind. I still didn't give the wind much thought. These things happen when you're aloft, after all. Fifteen minutes later, that all changed.

"Sir!" Simms, the airman at the bow called. "The *Vanguard* looks to be in distress!"

"I don't have your night sight, Simms. What do you see?"

"She's being tossed all over the place, sir. Like she's trying to ride through a huge sandstorm. It must be some kind of freak storm coming off the mountains over there."

"Can you take the wheel for a minute, dear, so I can take a look?"

Callan took the wheel and I joined Simms in the bow. The man tried his best to point out the floundering airship, but I still couldn't see it. Then something else caught my attention. Far above the ground—on the side of a mountain, no doubt—something flashed in the darkness.

Pointing toward the flashing, I asked Simms, "What can you make out from that flashing?"

The man peered in that direction for a few seconds. "I never seen anything like it, sir. It looks like a bunch of little lightning bolts shooting off in all directions."

A chill ran down my spine and I ran back to the controls yelling, "Land the ship *now*! And attach your safety lines!"

One wonderful thing about working with the Navy is the men don't stand around asking questions. The airmen leapt to their stations, venting gas from the envelope and operating ailerons to tilt the ship down.

Before taking the wheel, I fastened safety lines to Callan and then myself. Then I shoved the throttle forward and started a power dive for the ground. We were still five hundred feet in the air when a wall of wind slammed into us and capsized our airship.

I just managed to grab hold of Callan before we fell off the tilting deck of the tumbling airship. We fell for twenty feet before our safety lines snapped taught, stopping our fall with a painful jerk. I did my best to cushion Callan from the effects of the drop, but I felt the breath go out of her.

The wind howled around us as I tried to see what was happening. We hung between the airship's hull and its envelope, but that wouldn't last long. Even as I got my bearings, the envelope spun out from under us as the airship tried to right itself. More by luck than anything else, I was facing in the right direction as the ship's wooden hull spun out of the darkness at us. I just managed to bring my legs up so they took the brunt of the impact and kept the hull from smashing into Callan and me. One thing was certain—we would get battered to death if we couldn't secure ourselves somewhere.

"I need my hands free," I yelled at Callan. "Can you hold onto me?"

She nodded, tightly wrapping her arms around me. Once she was secure, I hauled hand-over-hand on my safety line and walked up the side of the hull. The airship continued tumbling as I did this, but the spinning actually helped me maintain my footing on the side of the ship.

Just as I reached the railing, the ship plunged straight down for a few seconds and we found ourselves dangling again. I didn't lose my grip on the safety line, though, so we found ourselves hanging five or six feet from the deck. Once again, the envelope pulled the ship back around and we crashed to the deck. Even as my breath blew out in a whoosh, I grabbed an inner railing. Holding us in place with one arm, I wrapped the other around Callan and pulled her to the railing, also.

The world continued spinning and the air was filled with flying debris. A belaying pin bounced painfully off of one of my kidneys and the tattered ends of broken ship's lines whipped at us, but at least we weren't out in the middle of it all.

Then Callan yelled, "David! Look aft!"

Rising flames lit the back of the airship and I realized the fire in the boiler had spilled free. I felt sure we'd be smashed into the ground before the fire reached us, but that wasn't exactly a comforting thought. I needed a chance to get my bearings so I could concoct some kind of plan, but the world was moving too fast for me to do that. So I decided to slow it down.

Boost!

My implant flooded my body with adrenaline and it was as if time slowed. All about me, bits and pieces of the airship flew as the ship continued its uncontrolled tumble, driven toward the ground by the raging windstorm. The fire, hungrily devouring the dry timber of the hull, cast illumination into the deep darkness of the desert. The ground was no more than a hundred feet below us and rushing up fast. But, if the ship kept tumbling the way it was, the envelope should hit first and cushion our landing. If I timed things just right...

"Grab onto me again!" I yelled at Callan as I drew a knife.

She did as I asked without question. Meanwhile, I threaded my left arm through the railing, more or less maintaining the hold anchoring us to the deck, then grabbed both of our safety lines with my now-free left hand. With a quick glance at the ground— no more than ten feet below the envelope by this time—I sawed through both safety lines.

Then the envelope hit the ground. The lines connecting the hull to the envelope—previously held taut by the spinning, slack-ened as the hull dropped and the envelope bounced up. I dropped my knife, jumped to my feet, and wrapped an arm around Callan. I dove for the outer railing and caught it with my right hand. With Boost-assisted strength, I swung the two of us over the railing and away from the tumbling, burning airship.

We plunged fifteen feet to the ground below. Boost gave me plenty of time to right ourselves, catch Callan with both arms, and land feet first. Letting my knees buckle—not that I really had any choice—I dropped and we rolled. And rolled. And rolled. My back smacked into something hard and rough. A few sharp points scraped my skin through my shirt.

Dropping Boost, I pulled my head back and examined Callan— only to find her doing the same thing to me.

"Are you okay?" we both asked and smiled in response to each other.

Sand and dust blew all around us, but we had managed to end up sheltered by the rock painfully jutting into my back and a small rise behind it. Grit still scoured our exposed skin, but it was nothing compared to the flaying we'd get if we moved away from our rock.

Through Callan's wildly blowing raven hair, I saw the last of the lines holding the hull to the envelope break. Freed from the weight of the hull, the envelope quickly swirled into the sky and out of sight. The hull continued rolling across the ground, scattering flaming wood all across the desert. Within seconds, our little airship was reduced to scrap.

We were stranded in the desert without food or water and hundreds of miles from the nearest city.

Callan and I huddled into our bare shelter from the slashing wind, hiding our faces against each other's chests. The gale shrieked so loudly talking was all but impossible. And then, it was gone, leaving behind an eerie quiet.

After a few seconds, I dared to look up. Dust slowly settled all around us, but that was all. "Let me take a quick look around, Callan. Stay down just in case the storm resumes."

"Stay close in case it does."

"You know me, dear—I never take chances."

Callan's snort turned into a cough as she cleared dust and sand from her lungs. Once I was certain Callan wasn't choking, I stood cautiously and stepped out of the small shelter afforded by the rocks. Light from the planetary ring lit the sky and shone down upon us, turning each dust mote into a tiny diamond sparkling in the air. Under other circumstances, I'd have found it beautiful.

"It's safe to get up," I said to Callan.

I brought my gaze back to the desert around us, searching for signs of other survivors. Burning timber lay scattered along the path our tumbling airship had taken. A much larger fire burned far off to my right. I felt certain that fire was the wreck of the *Vanguard*.

Callan put an arm around me. "What happened? I've never seen anything like that sudden wind nor heard tales of such."

Slipping my own arm around her, I said, "That's because it wasn't a natural storm."

Callan stiffened. "We don't have any weather control devices on Aashla. Our treaty with the Federation forbids them."

"We *didn't* have them—until two researchers killed the rest of their team and ran off with all sorts of high-tech equipment. I saw a small control sphere on the mountain just before I ordered the ship to land."

"Aren't satellites used to control the weather on Federation planets?"

"Yes, but you can also find smaller devices like the sphere. They're usually reserved for farm lands and other places with special weather requirements." My gaze returned to the distant fire. "And now they've been used to crash airships."

"But why?"

"I don't know, but I'm going to put a stop to it—and God help anyone who gets in my way."

FATE OF THE VANGUARD

Chris

"Did you really plan this search pattern, Chris?" Ensign Richie Parnell asked, his glass sweeping the area ahead and to starboard of our course. "And at the specific request of Her Highness?"

"Why? Do you think Lieutenant Anderson made that bit up to make me look good?" I asked in return, keeping my glass trained ahead and to port.

Richie snorted at the idea a ship's officer would do *anything* to make a mere ensign look good. "You've got me there. And the officers didn't get upset?"

"I don't think they were particularly happy at first, but they don't put idiots in charge of ships-of-the-line." I completed a sweep of my search arch and began the return scan. "They quickly recognized the superiority of my pattern. Captain Jorson even said 'good job, Ensign' when I finished."

"A captain complimenting an ensign—what is the world coming to?" Richie's voice held amusement, but also a little respect for my achievement. "And what about Princess Callan—is she as beautiful up close as she looks from a distance?"

"More beautiful, Richie. She is achingly, take-your-breath-away, gift-from-God, and put-angels-to-shame beautiful." I remembered

29

catching her as she fainted. Without thinking, I added, "And very soft."

In my peripheral vision, I saw Richie look at me in surprise and awe. "You *touched* her?"

"She fainted right into my arms." I couldn't keep the smug tone out of my voice. I also left out that I suspected her swoon was really feigned to draw me away from the grisly grave. "I assisted her to a seat in the shade and, on Dr. Mach's orders, catered to her every need until after dinner."

"Damn me, Chris, your life will never get any better than today," Richie said, giving a low whistle of appreciation. "You might as well retire now because your Naval career has already peaked."

"I'd like to think I can make some small contribution to the Navy in the future," I said. "Besides catching swooning princesses, that is."

"Right you are, Ensign Marlow," Lieutenant Anderson said, his voice right behind me. "Ensign Parnell, get your eye back to that glass or your next contribution to the Navy will involve potatoes and a peeling knife. Do I make myself clear?"

"Aye aye, sir!" we both barked.

"Have either of you spotted anything?" the lieutenant asked.

"No, sir," Richie said.

I saw movement on the side of the mountain ahead of us. When I realized it was just trees blowing in the wind, I almost dismissed it. But the trees were bending very sharply, so I spoke up.

"Check the side of the mountain, sir. By the look of the trees, a very strong wind is blowing over there."

I heard the snap as Lieutenant Anderson opened his own spyglass. "Good eye, Ensign Marlow. Prepare the crew for rough weather. I'll inform the Captain."

Richie and I scrambled aloft, calling, "Prepare for rough weather. Attach safety lines!"

Up and down the ship, the officers and senior airmen took up the shout. I lost sight of Richie as we approached our duty stations on opposite sides of the envelope. I looped my own safety line through the rigging and tied it off. As the airman to my left double-checked my line, I did the same for the airman to my right.

"Prepare for high winds, men," I called over the already-rising gusts. "I think we're in for quite a blow."

The words were barely out of my mouth when the full force of the wind struck our side of the envelope. The *Vanguard* heeled to starboard so sharply we found the side of the envelope beneath our feet. I heard cries of surprise and fear from the men up and down the envelope.

Two men were too slow fastening their safety lines and were blown from their perches. One of them was lucky—two of his mates caught his safety line and pulled him back to his post. The other poor soul tumbled across the envelope and over the edge. Mercifully, the howling wind covered the scream as he fell to his death far below.

After that, we were busy watching for rips in the envelope and patching them before they could widen and threaten the entire ship. Despite the horrific conditions and the wildly swinging envelope, the men maintained discipline and performed their jobs admirably.

I alternated watching for rips with watching the *Vanguard's* progress as the Captain struggled to bring her safely to the ground. After what felt like an eternity, the ground appeared and rushed toward us with frightening speed.

I shouted at the top of my voice, hoping the men heard me over the wind. "Prepare to cut safety lines! The Captain will release the envelope as soon as we're grounded, so drop off as soon as you're free."

Carefully gauging the time until we grounded, I waited as long as possible before shouting, "Cut lines!"

All around me, knives slashed at safety lines. I raised my own knife to cut my line, only to lose my grip on the rigging. As I dropped to the end of my safety line, I heard the grinding and cracking of wood as the hull smashed into the ground. I saw my men dropping free around me as I struggled to grab the handle of my knife as it danced at the end of the lanyard tying it to my wrist. Just as I caught hold of it, the envelope blew free from the hull and tumbled across the desert.

Flung about like a doll at the end of a string, I struggled to cut my safety line and free myself from the tumbling deathtrap that was the envelope. I bounced off the envelope once and had the entire thing press me into the ground another time. And then I managed to saw through my line. The last thing I saw was the ground rushing beneath me. Then I struck the hard-packed desert floor and everything went black.

UNEXPECTED AID

David

Callan nodded, fatigue etched on her lovely face. "I guess six years between life-threatening adventures is the best I can hope for. We start by searching for survivors, I assume?"

As we set out along the path our airship took as it bounced across the desert, I said, "You know, Martin or Rupor would have met my declaration with some kind of affirmation—'We will make them pay for this' or whatever. Probably something a lot better since they're both much better with words than I am. Even Nist would have given me a fierce grin."

Callan patted me on the shoulder. "When this is over, I'll step aside graciously if you want to marry one of them. But if you want some kind of affirmation..." Callan kissed me gently. "Don't die. And to show I'm a fair-minded woman, I promise I'll do my best to follow my own instructions."

I took an extra few seconds to extend the kiss. "Now *that* is what I call an affirmation!"

It was the last sweet and gentle moment we had together that night.

We found Simms first. He lay tangled in a pile of wreckage from our airship, his neck bent at an impossible angle and sightless eyes staring up into the night sky. I closed his eyes as Callan recited a short prayer for the dead. I wanted to cover his body with debris to protect it from scavengers, but we couldn't afford the time as long as there was a chance of finding survivors.

We found the other two airmen from our ship a few minutes later, both also dead. With the flames from the *Vanguard* flickering in the distance, we still couldn't spare the time to protect the bodies. Both times Callan spoke prayers for the dead and then we set off for the distant wreck.

By some miracle, we stumbled across an intact water bottle before we got clear of our airship's debris. The warm water cleared the dust from our mouths and throats and revived us both a bit. Even so, within thirty minutes we were supporting each other as we trudged across the rough terrain.

My mind tried to wander during the trek and each time I forced it back to consider our situation. Three airships took part in the search. Obviously, the windstorm destroyed our ship and the *Vanguard*, but what of the *Tercel?* The search pattern Marlow devised sent that warship well away from the mountains and the weather sphere.

Did the sphere possess sufficient power to extend its windstorm far enough out to get the other ship? If so, it almost certainly crashed, too, leaving the messenger ship as our only hope for eventual rescue. If the *Tercel* was beyond the storm, it would come steaming to our rescue the moment Captain Jorson figured out what happened to us. And probably get blown out of the sky by another windstorm once it was inside the sphere's range.

After wrestling with possibilities and plans for half an hour, I finally decided to assume the ship was down and Callan and I were on our own. That's when Callan pulled me away from my contemplations.

"David, look!" She pointed toward the flaming hulk that had once been the *Vanguard.*

Backlit by the fire, I saw figures moving around the wreck. Some of the crew had survived! We were much too far away to even try shouting, but some of our exhaustion fell away, our steps lightened, and we picked up the pace.

We watched men dart about the flames and sometimes into the flames. Many times the distant silhouettes emerged from the burning wreck carrying or supporting others. It stirred my heart to watch these brave airmen risk their lives to save their shipmates. Callan and I tried counting figures, hoping to get an idea how many of the original four hundred crewmen had survived, but it was an impossible task. The best we could determine was that many—far too many—members of the crew were dead or trapped inside the burning wreck.

On and on we marched and slowly, ever so slowly, we drew closer to the brightly lit scene of destruction and heroism. Our aching feet carried us, as we ignored our weary legs, to the safety of bright light and greater numbers.

We were but half a mile from the downed airship when everything changed. Pops and cracks sounded in the distance, which we believed came from the burning hull. Then we saw tiny silhouettes falling and not rising again and realized something worse was going on. Suddenly, a mass of figures charged in from the darkness, running in a peculiar short-legged stride I recognized.

"Trogs!" Callan cried, recognizing the new figures as quickly as I had.

I watched one of the trogs stop and raise what looked like a stick to his shoulder. A crack sounded and an airman fifty feet away pitched backward and lay still.

"Dear God," I whispered, "they're armed with blaster rifles!"

I tensed, preparing to charge into the fray far ahead of me. Callan's hand caught my forearm and pulled me back. She wasn't strong enough to stop me—I could have easily shaken off her hand —but Callan wasn't trying to stop me physically.

"You won't reach them in time to do anything, David," she told me with quiet force. "All you'll do is make me a widow and leave your children without a father."

The tension flowed out of my muscles as the wisdom behind

her words overcame my natural tendency toward action. I nodded, accepting her counsel even as I looked around us for some form of cover. Half a mile separated us from the slaughter and the bright light from the fire surely destroyed the trogs' night vision but was the band attacking the *Vanguard's* crew the only trog force in the area?

Callan spotted a small patch of scrub brush off to our right and we hurried to it. Pushing into the center of the mass of stiff branches and prickly leaves, we discovered the brush grew over a shallow depression. During rare rain storms, water probably pooled here, making it an ideal place for the hardy bushes to grow. For us, the depression let us lie down beneath the lowest branches, providing even better cover than we'd originally hoped for.

By the time we settled in, the distant crack of blaster fire fell silent. Guttural trog shouts floated to us across the desert. Every now and then a human cry or shout reached our ears, as well. Some of the crew still lived, at least. I would have given a lot for one glance at the scene next to the burning hull. It seemed likely the trogs were taking the survivors prisoner—we would hear more men shouting if the trogs were simply executing them—but I couldn't be sure without at least one look.

My chances of getting a quick glance and dropping back into cover struck me as very good, so I carefully brought my knees up under me. Callan gave me a quizzical look. I replied by pointing up then pantomimed looking around. She considered it for a couple of seconds and nodded once.

Then we both nearly jumped out of our skins when we heard footsteps approaching our position. Silently, I lay flat again then we both went as still as stones. Our hopes of hearing the voices of fellow Mordanians were crushed when a trog spoke from no more than ten feet away. He was right next to our hiding place.

Another trog replied to the first one and the two conversed for something like three years. My implant said it was only half a minute, but it sure felt thousands of times longer than that. Finally, the first trog gave what had to be an order. The second trog gave a single grunt in reply. Seconds after that, a spear pierced the bushes above us, coming within five or six inches of Callan's hip.

We both carefully rolled from our sides onto our backs, getting as far from the probing spears as possible. Another spear thrust into the bushes from another direction, stopping seven or eight inches above my head. Five times the spears thrust through the bushes and five times the spears missed us. The closest stopped less than two inches from my leg.

Unaware of the depression that protected us from their spears, the trogs were soon satisfied no one hid in the bushes. The leader growled a quick command and the patrol headed in the direction we'd come from—doubtless to check our wrecked airship for survivors. Of course, they wouldn't find any. Nor would they have any way of knowing we had been on the airship.

Callan and I waited a full five minutes before we even allowed ourselves to take more than shallow breaths. Then Callan rolled toward me and laid her head on my shoulder. I felt the warm splash of tears as she softly recited the prayer for the dead in its entirety. I just held her close and, equally quietly, joined in the prayer.

When the prayer came to an end, she surprised me with one addition. "Lord, watch over the survivors and keep them close in Your sight until David and I can rescue them."

I waited a few seconds until I was sure she was done. "Dear, what was that last part of your prayer?"

"I think it was pretty obvious, darling. And are you going to honestly tell me you weren't planning on rescuing those crewmen?"

"Of course I'm going to rescue those men. It's the 'David and I' part I question."

"I know you've already considered the chances of a rescue party coming for us any time soon, David." Callan held up a hand and ticked off on her fingers. "The *Sky Runner* is only a few hours into its two-day flight to the closest Federation consulate and has no idea what's happened here. We know the *Vanguard* is wrecked. It's a safe bet the *Tercel* is wrecked, too. If it wasn't, we'd have heard her engines as Captain Jorson came to investigate. No doubt we'd have been subjected to another windstorm, as well. Did I miss anything?"

"Yes, there are heavily armed trogs patrolling the area and guarding the survivors," I replied.

Callan bestowed a smile on me as if I'd just helped prove her point. "Call it three days until rescuers arrive." She raised her eyebrows and I nodded in agreement. "We have no water, no food, no supplies except the sword at your side." Without eyebrow prompting, I nodded again and she continued. "Now comes the hard part, David. What do you think my odds of survival are if I stay out here all alone?"

Instinctively, I opened my mouth to spout something reassuring, paused, and then closed my mouth again. I quickly ran through all of the options in my mind. Placing my hand gently on Callan's cheek, I said, "I want nothing more than to keep you safe, Callan."

She kissed me softly. "I know, David, and the best way you can do that is to take me with you. Left alone out here, I'll probably die of thirst, get caught by trogs, or killed by a tammar or something. If I'm with you, you have an extra pair of eyes to keep watch and another brain to help solve problems."

I sighed. "It'll be extremely dangerous—but no worse than leaving you alone in the desert."

Callan kissed me a second time. "That wasn't so hard, was it darling?"

My glare had no effect on her, so I gave up and turned to making plans. My wife was right about one thing—having another brain working on the problem helped a lot. Half an hour later, we had our plan. Details were sparse, but I reiterated the plan anyway to make sure we were both on the same page.

"We're going to take turns sleeping and keeping watch until that trog patrol returns. If it's still dark, we slip out of this brush and follow them at a distance. If it's light, we watch the way they go and then try to pick up their trail once they're out of sight."

Callan nodded and I continued. "We can't plan much beyond that because we don't know what the situation will be at the trog village. So we play it by ear after that."

Then we settled in to wait. I took first watch, letting Callan catch some much needed sleep. We traded off a couple of hours later and traded again two hours after that. Midway through my watch, I heard guttural conversation coming our way and woke Callan.

Dawn was still hours away, so we waited quietly for the trogs to reach us. They passed no more than fifty feet from our hiding place. Five minutes later, Callan and I carefully pushed free of the scrub brush. Keeping low, we set off on the trail of the trogs.

Had Callan and I been well-rested and unconcerned about being spotted, our longer legs would have made it easy to keep pace with the loping trogs. Instead, they drew steadily farther and farther ahead of us as our exhaustion and caution slowed us down. By the time the trogs reached the foot of the mountain before us, they were half a mile ahead.

We dropped behind some bushes in case one of the trogs chose that moment to look behind them. Callan's head hung down and she gasped for breath. Sweat made tracks in the thin coating of dust on her face. She swiped a hand across her brow and brushed at her cheeks, smearing the dust.

Without looking up, she said, "I'm worn out, David. Go on without me. You can come back when you've found the trog village."

I took a moment to master my own ragged breathing then shook my head. "You've already convinced me that staying together is the safest thing to do. I'm not about to ignore the advice of the heir to my kingdom's throne. That mountain looks like one big pile of loose stones and the trogs are leaving quite a trail behind them."

Callan lifted her head and straightened her back to peer over the bushes. Slumping back, she asked, "So we're going to rest for a while?"

"Yes."

"Good. You take first watch." Callan toppled my way and settled her head into my lap. Seconds later, her breathing deepened and her face relaxed as she fell asleep.

I took a few minutes to survey the desert around us. Nothing moved except the band of trogs trudging up the mountain ahead of us. I gently rearranged Callan into a more comfortable position and pulled the hair away from her face. Despite being covered in grime—not to mention giving birth to two children and enduring the stress of taking the lead in guiding Aashla toward membership in the Terran Federation—she still took my breath away. She brought sanity and meaning and deep, abiding love into my life. There was nothing I would not do and nothing I would not give to keep her safe.

A voice jerked me from my reverie. "Is Her Highness hurt?"

I looked up to find Ensign Marlow crouched fifteen feet away. His uniform was torn and covered in dirt and blood. Dried blood tracked down his face from a gash on his forehead. The lad looked like death warmed over and yet his first concern was for his princess.

I waved the boy closer. "She's fine, Ensign, just worn out—as I'm sure you are. Why don't you lay down over here and get some sleep, too?"

Marlow took a good look around before sitting down beside me. He strove for a neutral expression as he said, "I should take watch and let you sleep, sir."

"Meaning I'm so tired you were able to sneak up on me, so it would be safer for you to take watch."

Shock crossed Marlow's face—probably as much because I'd spoken the thought aloud as that I'd guessed correctly. "I'd *never* say such a thing, sir!"

"I know, Ensign," I chuckled, "that's why *I* said it. And you're right, too, though it pains me to admit it. I had to Boost as our airship crashed. I haven't done that in years and it's taken a toll on me."

Marlow's eyes lit. "Oh, I wish I'd been there to see that!"

"I'm glad you weren't." A hurt expression flashed across Marlow's face before I continued, "It was a violent crash that no one else survived. If you'd been there, you'd probably be dead, too."

"Oh." The Ensign thought on that for a few seconds. "Then I thank God you were there to save Her Highness."

"You and me both," I replied. "What's your first name, Ensign?"

"Um, Chris, sir."

"Christopher Marlow?" I smiled broadly.

"Is there something wrong with my name, sir?" Chris's tone grew just a tad prickly.

"Not at all, Chris. You just happen to share the same name as an ancient playwright who lived on Terra centuries before mankind found his way into space."

"Oh." Chris thought on this for a moment. "Were his plays any good, sir?"

"I honestly don't know. I've never seen one performed, but his name has survived for thousands of years. That should tell you something. Also, when it's just the three of us please call me David." At Chris's shocked expression, I added, "I can make that an order if it will make you feel any better. And my wife will insist you call her Callan."

That was too much for poor Chris. He sat bolt upright and said, "I couldn't do that, sir! Er, David. Sir. It wouldn't be right for a commoner to be so familiar with a member of the royal family!"

"Who told you that?" The sleepy voice came from my lap as Callan cracked a single eye open and looked up at Chris.

"My mother, Your Highness. She always taught me to be respectful to my betters."

Callan turned her open eye on me. "This one is going to take some work, darling. Remind me to get right on that—after I sleep for another year or two."

Callan's eye slid closed again. She was asleep in seconds.

I looked back at the young Ensign. "When did you sleep last, Chris?"

"I was off-shift at the beginning of the search, sir." At my raised eyebrow, Chris sighed. "David. So I had several hours of sleep before starting my watch an hour or so before that strange wind-storm hit."

I rearranged myself to lie down next to Callan, all the while cradling her head in my arms. "The storm was strange because it was manmade."

Chris's eyes widened. "But that's against all of the treaties!"

My eyelids dragged themselves down over my eyes. "Yes, it most definitely is."

The next time I opened my eyes, the sun was three-quarters of the way up toward noon. Desert heat surrounded us but did not beat directly down upon me. At some point, someone dragged me into the meager shade provided by the bush. I rolled onto my back and found Callan sitting beside me, taking advantage of some of the shade, as well.

"Good morning, darling." She bent over and kissed me.

I sat up and looked around. The wreck of the *Vanguard* still smoked as the last of the fires burned themselves out. Other than the rising smoke, nothing else moved. The smoke, though, told a tale I definitely did not care for.

"Where is Chris? You didn't send him running into the desert in a panic over the idea of calling you by your first name, did you?"

"Of course not, David. He insisted on scouting ahead and, once I was certain he wouldn't do anything foolish, I allowed him to go."

"How, pray tell, does one convince a teenage boy *not* to do something foolish?"

"I teared up a bit at the way his mother would react when I visited her to tell her of her son's untimely death."

"And that did the trick?"

"I may have also mentioned two or three young ladies I felt certain would find him fascinating, should he live long enough to return to the palace with us."

I shook my head in admiration. "You play dirty, my dear."

"I play to win, darling. In this case, winning means surviving." Callan rose to her feet and I followed suit. "I told Chris that we'd follow if you awoke before he returned."

We set off toward the rock-strewn mountain, that proved just as difficult to scale as I thought it would. The trogs' trail proved dead easy to follow, though. It headed up at an angle and out of sight around a pile of large boulders. Reaching the boulders, we found Chris on his way back.

"Did you find the trog village, Chris?" I asked.

To my surprise, Chris shook his head. "The trail doesn't go to a village, David. It ends at a strange cave."

"What's in the cave?"

"That's what is so strange, sir," Chris said. "The cave is empty."

"Did you go into the cave?" I asked.

"Of course, sir, though not very far." Chris bowed slightly in Callan's direction. "I promised Her Highness I would be careful."

"I told you to call me Callan," my wife gently admonished the boy. "And thank you for honoring your promise."

"How long did you stay in the cave? Did you give your eyes time to adjust to the darkness?"

"Yes, sir. I stayed inside for five minutes. The cave is less than thirty feet deep and only ten to fifteen feet wide." Chris shrugged. "I don't think I missed anything."

A trog trail leading up to an empty cave struck me as far-fetched in the extreme. As a race, trogs are very direct with an almost in-your-face approach to life. That lack of subtlety had led humans on Aashla to assume the trogs were simply stupid. Since Aashla made contact with the wider galaxy, properly equipped researchers have shed a lot of light on the race. The short version is that trogs are genetically disinclined to such deception. The two missing human researchers, on the other hand, were probably quite skilled at deception.

"I don't doubt your observations at all, Chris, but I'd like to check out the cave for myself." I motioned back the way the Ensign had come from. "Would you lead us to it?"

Chris snapped off a salute, spun about, and all but marched down the path. Smiling and shaking her head, Callan took my hand and we followed the boy.

"He's quite an earnest young officer, our Chris." Callan leaned close to me and kept her voice low. "Doesn't he remind you a bit of Milo?"

"If by 'remind' you mean 'is the complete opposite of' then I'm right there with you. Though, like Milo, he does have the good taste to be smitten with you."

"Oh pish and tosh, David. I'm just an old married woman from Chris's point of view."

"If I may be so bold," Chris said over his shoulder, "Her Highness does herself an injustice. I have already earned the envy of a fellow ensign for yesterday. If the rest knew I was serving you directly... Let's just say I won't have to pay for drinks the next time we're in a tavern."

I grinned. "Okay, *now* he reminds me of Milo!"

"You heard everything we said, Chris?" Callan asked.

"Yes, Your Highness. An officer in the Royal Navy must be aware of all that goes on around him—especially the mutterings of the men in his command." Chris looked back at us. "I'm also the youngest of seven children. Keen hearing is a survival trait in such a large family."

"Perhaps I should whisper my most intimate comments into your ear, dear," I said to Callan. "I'd hate to embarrass the Ensign."

The back of Chris's neck turned red and his back stiffened. "I would never intentionally listen to a private conversation, sir—especially not one between a husband and wife!"

"We know, Chris." Callan quickened her pace and put an arm around the boy's shoulders. "You have our complete trust."

I watched Chris's right arm twitch and almost wrap itself around Callan's waist. The lad caught himself, though, and turned to see if I had spotted his almost-move with my wife. I quickly looked off into the distance. The boy had enough to worry about right now without worrying about attracting my disapproval, as well. Seventeen was nearly half a lifetime ago for me, but I still remembered what it was like.

Then we rounded a turn and spotted the cave entrance less than fifty feet ahead of us. It was right out in the open where anyone walking the trail would see it. That didn't mean much, seeing how the mountain was at the edge of a desert. Probably only a handful of people in the history of Aashla ever laid eyes on the cave mouth.

"You two wait here," I said, striding past them. "Ensign Marlow, if anything happens to me your one duty is to get Princess Callan to safety. Is that clear?"

Marlow responded, "Absolutely clear, sir."

"Aren't you being a tad melodramatic, David?" Callan asked.

I gave Callan a brief but tight hug. "No, I'm not, Callan. Besides, you ought to be used to it by now."

"It's been six years since our last adventure, darling. I'd rather hoped you'd have gotten over your 'Captain of the Princess's Guard' fixation."

"And risk having Rob come back to haunt me? No thank you!"

"Fine, darling. I promise to do everything Ensign Marlow tells me to do." Callan pecked me on the mouth. "Do you feel better now?"

"Immensely."

I trotted over to the cave entrance, stopping outside and listening. Once I was satisfied all was quiet inside the cave, I slipped through the opening and stepped to the side of the entrance and out of the direct light. My eyes quickly adjusted to the darkness but I still waited a half a minute after that before moving deeper into the cave.

There wasn't much to see inside. A lot of rocks—ranging from fist-sized to ones three or four feet across—were scattered over the floor. Near the back, one huge rock leaned against the left side of the cave. That was the only possible hiding place in the cave, though I dutifully checked all around the larger rocks on the floor as I worked my way to the boulder in the back.

Once I reached the leaning boulder, I squatted down and looked into the space between it and the cave wall. It was even darker than normal under there and I almost stuck my hand in to check the wall. Then I remembered the poisonous many-legged desert creature that almost bit Callan during my very first night on Aashla. I drew my sword instead and tapped along the wall, neither finding an opening nor flushing out any creatures.

I slowly walked around the boulder, pushing against it to make sure it wasn't precariously balanced. The thing was firmly wedged in place, so I stepped around the far side of the rock and into the small space between it and the back of the cave. I was so certain I'd find nothing besides cave wall that I actually jumped back a couple of feet when I spotted the entrance to another cave hidden behind the boulder. More surprisingly, dim light flickered deep inside that cave.

BRAVE SACRIFICE

David

A few feet past the entrance, the tunnel took a sharp turn to the right and headed deeper into the mountain. Wanting to get a look around that turn, I sidled into the new cave quietly and carefully, keeping my chest pressed against the right-hand wall. I cocked my head, alert for the slightest indication that someone was coming. That is what saved me.

I heard the sound of fabric against rock, the barest of unnatural susurrations, but it told me I wasn't alone. Without a second thought, I dropped into a backward somersault. Just as I tucked into the roll, a trog jumped into view. He fired his blaster rifle from the hip and the bolt ricocheted off the wall I'd been pressed against half a second before.

The barrel of the rifle tracked my way as I came up out of my roll. Planting both feet against the left wall, I leveled my sword and lunged at the trog's chest. My blue-skinned opponent brought his blaster rifle up in an attempt to parry my thrust. He deflected my blade up and away from his chest—and into his throat! Hot blood sprayed from his neck as my sword ripped veins and arteries.

Gurgling, the trog dropped the rifle and clawed at his throat in a futile effort to stem the fatal flow of blood. He stumbled forward, eyes wide and glaring at me. The trog dropped to his knees then pitched face-first onto the cave floor.

Snatching up the blaster rifle, I waited for fifteen tense seconds but no more trogs leapt to the attack nor did I hear shouts or cries of alarm from deeper in the cave. Confident I was alone, I cleaned my sword on the trog's tunic and sheathed it. Leaning the blaster rifle against the wall, I picked up the heavy corpse and draped an arm over one shoulder and a leg over the other. Careful with my ungainly burden, I grabbed the stock of the blaster rifle and staggered back the way I'd come.

I'd been in the cave for no more than ten minutes, but the sunlight was dazzling and felt almost unnatural in comparison. Callan and Chris rushed to help me when I emerged. Chris looked particularly pale, staring at the dead trog with troubled eyes.

"I swear I didn't see the trog, sir!" Chris said as he took some of the trog's weight off my shoulders.

"Are you all right, David?" Callan asked, her eyes flicking all over me in search of any wounds.

"I'm fine, Callan. All of the fresh blood on me is blue." I gave an encouraging smile at Chris. "I know you didn't see the trog, Chris. There's another cave branching off behind that big boulder at the back of the cave. This guy was in there, probably standing guard. You couldn't have seen him."

Despite my words, Chris looked down, refusing to meet my gaze. "I should have found that cave."

"You most certainly should *not* have, Ensign Marlow!" Callan snapped, her sharp tone catching the lad by surprise. "You were under direct orders from a member of the royal family to be careful and avoid unnecessary risks—such as exploring a cave by yourself."

"Before you lay into him further, dear," I said, handing the blaster rifle to Callan, "could we please find a place to stash this body? It's rather heavy."

"We're on a mountain, David. I'm sure we can find dozens of

places to hide the corpse." Callan looked about quickly before leading us upslope. "Why did you even bother bringing it with you?"

"I don't see any point in advertising our presence any more than necessary."

"Won't the trogs figure out what happened when they discover all the blood inside the cave?" Chris gasped, struggling with his half of the heavy burden.

"I'm going to go back and scatter dirt over all the blood," I replied. "It might make a particularly dim trog think this guy came outside to relieve himself or something."

Callan pointed beyond a jumble of rocks. "There's a steep scree over here. If you toss the body down it, it should be pretty easy to push more rocks down on top of it."

We did as instructed then spent the next thirty minutes pushing rocks down to cover the body. It wasn't perfect, but it was far better than I'd hoped for.

When we were finished, the three of us settled down to rest in the shade of an overhang that was out of sight from the cave entrance. I took that time to take a look at the blaster rifle. A cursory examination showed the rifle wasn't complete—much of the outer covering was missing, for instance.

The missing pieces didn't affect the rifle's function, but they might affect how long it functioned. The covering existed to protect the more delicate inner workings from the elements. Without constant cleaning, dust and sand could completely disable the internal electronics. Looking at this one sample, cleaning hadn't been high on its owner's list of things to do.

"Are you going to explain all of those murmured comments and grunts you're making, David?" Callan asked.

"Sorry, dear, I wasn't aware I was making them."

"You never are, darling." She smiled fondly to make sure I understood this fell under the category of 'endearing trait' rather than 'annoying habit'. "So, explanations?"

"First, the rifle is rather crude by galactic standards. It looks like whoever built this repurposed a lot of electronics to function as a blaster rifle. The Federation restricts weapon components for this very reason, but someone quite clever figured out a way around it." I pointed to different interior components of the rifle. "These are quite common electronic parts—you can probably find them at every Federation research station on Aashla—but they've been combined in such a way that they work entirely differently than designed. That explains how those two rogue researchers got this stuff past Federation inspectors."

Callan and Chris exchanged a look before Callan said, "We non-technical lost colonists will happily take you at your word. That explains the muttering. What about the grunts?"

"That was just me expressing professional disdain for the trog's weapon maintenance. This thing is filthy. Dirt can mess up the operation of weapons as simple as crossbows. It's about a hundred times worse in something like this rifle. I'm surprised the thing works at all."

Callan patted my arm. "Well, hadn't you better get started cleaning it?"

"You know me so well, dear."

Chris leaned in, keen interest written on his face. "Will you teach me how to clean this weapon, sir?"

"Sure. And how many times do I have to tell you to call—"

Suddenly, a trog voice rose in the distance. I didn't have to understand the language to recognize the tone of someone issuing commands. The trogs must have discovered their guard was missing.

I handed the blaster rifle to Callan and whispered, "Both of you keep quiet and stay out of sight."

Moving with caution on the scree, I crept up to the small crest over which we'd carried the trog's body. Trog feet crunched in the loose stone outside the cave entrance. I tried to gauge their numbers based on the noise the trogs made, but it proved well beyond me. I turned onto my left side, closed my left eye, and carefully peered over the brow with my right eye. A hundred feet below me, something like two dozen trogs milled around the entrance to the cave. One stood aloof—their leader, no doubt—watching two more trogs scanning the ground for tracks of some kind.

Chris and I had left obvious tracks as we lugged the corpse up the hill but now our tracks were almost entirely gone. Callan must have smoothed out the stones behind us. Being far lighter than the combined weight of two men and a dead body, she'd managed to walk over the same terrain leaving hardly a sign of her passage. Would that prove enough to send the trogs off in another direction?

Two agonizing minutes crept by before the trackers returned to the leader and reported. He considered their report for a moment before issuing orders to his patrol. All but four trogs fell in behind the trackers and their leader, who led them off the way we'd originally come.

I quietly released a breath I hadn't realized I was holding. Four guards still blocked our only known path away from our hiding place, but I felt certain we could take out those four if it proved absolutely necessary. With the same caution I'd used ascending to the crest, I returned to Callan and Chris.

"A good twenty trogs are following the wrong trail in search of us." I took Callan's hand and kissed it. "That's all thanks to you, dear. If you hadn't covered our tracks in the rocks, we'd be prisoners of the trogs right now."

Chris gave me a puzzled look. "Didn't you battle at least that many trogs when you first met Her Highness? If you Boosted, surely you could handle them without any problems!"

"You're a smart lad, Chris," I chided gently. "Stop thinking of me as some invincible hero and start thinking about what's different between then and now."

"Well, you're older now," Chris said more to himself than to me, "so that might slow you down a bit. But even if it did, Her Highness or I could lend supporting fire with this blaster rifle and-. Oh." The Ensign shook his head in disgust. "The trogs have blaster rifles, too. Even Boosted, there's no way you could dodge that much massed fire."

I gave Chris an encouraging smile. "Exactly."

"How could I be so stupid? I should have realized that from the beginning!"

Callan placed a gentle hand on the boy's shoulder. "I know quite a few Naval officers who wouldn't have figured it out as quickly as you did. Why are you so hard on yourself over something little like this?"

Chris just shook his head and turned away from us to stare at the rock giving us shelter. Callan turned a questioning gaze my way. I had an idea what was bothering the boy, but only because of a comment from Dr. Mach, the expedition's surgeon. Chris was plenty smart, but I got the idea he felt his intelligence was his only asset and put enormous pressure on himself to be quick on the uptake.

"You know, I remember my first Scout Academy expedition when I was a cadet. I had all the coursework down cold and was certain I was going to set some kind of record for the best first cadet cruise ever." Chris didn't turn around, but his head shifted slightly so he could hear my words better. "I was so busy imagining the honors that would be heaped on me that I hardly even paid attention during the tour of the ship and only noted my duty station in passing. After all, it was a three-week cruise. I'd have plenty of time to memorize the ship's layout. Can you guess what happened, Chris?"

The boy nodded. "Right after the tour ended, an alarm sounded and you were ordered to report to your duty station."

"Yep. I was completely lost. When I asked another cadet for help, he told me to follow someone else assigned to the same station. It was good advice and better than I deserved—only I didn't know which cadets were assigned to the same station. When the officers began their inspection tour, I was still running around hoping to stumble into my station. Instead I stumbled into the Captain—literally. I knocked him flat on his butt."

This revelation drew a look of horrified fascination from Chris. "They didn't throw you out of the academy for that?"

"No, they just gave me all the worst cadet assignments for the rest of the year." I smiled ruefully at the boy. "Smart people make mistakes, Chris. Smarter people learn from their mistakes and move on."

"What if being smart is all you've got?"

"Then you're selling yourself short!" Callan insisted. "In the last two days, you've survived the wreck of your airship, avoided being killed or captured by trogs, found David and me, tracked the trogs to their hidden lair, and helped David hide a body. Not to mention catching me when I was overcome by the heat yesterday afternoon."

"I know you were just pretending yesterday, Your Highness."

Callan raised an eyebrow imperiously. "A princess never *pretends*, Ensign. She chooses alternative means to accomplish her goal. But if you knew, why didn't you protest and remain with the men at the grave site?"

Chris blushed furiously and ducked his head.

Taking pity on the boy—after all, I understood the appeal of wrapping my arms around Callan—I said, "A gentleman never questions a lady's request for assistance."

"Then it was done quite gallantly, Ensign, as have been your actions since then. I shall have stern words for anyone who would cast aspersions on you or your behavior."

After that little discussion, we settled down to rest while waiting for the trog patrol to wander farther from the cave entrance. I did my best to clean the blaster rifle during that time but could only blow out the dust and brush at the sand with my fingers. I judged the gun in more serviceable condition when I was done, though the rifle was far from clean.

An hour later, the three of us crept to the crest to spy out the situation. Four trogs milled about the cave entrance, with three relaxing and one keeping an actual watch. None of them was looking our way. Assuming the rifle's sights were true, four quick blaster shots should clear our way. I was just lining up the first shot when Chris caught my shoulder and shook his head.

"The patrol is returning," he whispered.

Thank God for the boy's young ears because several seconds passed before I heard the patrol. Shortly, they came into sight and rejoined the four guards. Trog voices rose in discussion for a minute or so, then the leader turned and looked up the slope toward us. I ducked out of sight before he saw me but it didn't matter. The leader issued an order. Right after that we heard the unmistakable sound of trogs climbing up the slope.

I motioned for Callan and Chris to back away from the crest of our part of the mountain. We slithered down as quickly and quietly as possible. Once the trogs couldn't see us if we stood, I rose to my feet and unbuckled my sword belt.

"What are you doing, David?" Callan whispered, her voice barely audible above the sound of the trogs slogging through the scree on the opposite slope.

"Trade swords with me, Chris." I held my sword belt out to the Ensign. "There is no way I'm letting Rob's sword fall into trog hands."

Callan scowled at me and her voice took on a brittle edge. "Darling, I asked you a question."

Chris froze, his head swinging back and forth between the two of us, his sword belt only partially unbuckled. I shook my sword belt under his nose.

"*Now*, Ensign!" Turning back to Callan, I said, "I'm going to distract the trogs and give you and Chris a chance to either hide or find another way out of here."

"Let's find that hiding place or another way out—together. All three of us," Callan pleaded.

"This is who I am, Callan, and this is what I do. And you knew that when you married me," I said, smiling. "Remember, a kingdom needs a monarch and it needs an heir. Your father is safe, thank God, and I'm about to ensure his heir is safe, too."

Callan nodded reluctantly, wrapping her arms around me for a quick, perhaps final, hug. That's when Chris dropped his sword belt and bolted back up the slope!

"I'll distract the trogs. You must protect Princess Callan!"

I grabbed for Chris's arm but the boy timed his break perfectly. With Callan's arms entwined around me, I couldn't lunge after Chris. My fingertips brushed against his sleeve and then the boy was out of reach.

The flash of sunlight momentarily blinded me and memories of another sixteen-year-old boy flooded my mind. I saw a pinnace flash past, meters above me and heard Milo's last words.

"You're not dying if I can help it! Take care of Kim for me."

My vision cleared and I saw Chris raising his arms as he reached the top of the slope. Much as I wanted to charge after the boy and protect him, my duty lay with Callan. Honoring Chris's last plea, I turned away from the Ensign and dragged Callan around the rocks and out of sight of the top of the slope.

A blaster rifle fired, followed closely by a second. Even as I carefully led Callan down the steep scree we'd used to hide the trog body, I waited for Chris's last cry as the bolts blasted the life out of him. Instead, the trog leader shouted something. No third shot came and I realized one of the two shots must have killed the boy instantly.

Tears welled up in my eyes and I harshly crushed the emotions that drew them forth. With no idea how long Callan and I had before the trogs investigated further, I simply couldn't afford the luxury of emotions, much less tears. I gave Callan a quick glance and saw her wipe at her eyes, but also saw a look of grim determination settle over her face. Between the two of us, we would make the trogs pay dearly for Chris's life.

We slipped and slid past the point where the trog's corpse was buried under the stones. A dozen feet later we reached the boulders piled at the bottom of the scree. Callan and I quickly scanned the area, hoping for a narrow passage between boulders, and came up empty. Far away, the trog leader issued more orders and I had to assume he was ordering his warriors onward.

I dragged Callan off to the side of the scree. "Get down on the ground, Callan, and I'll cover you with stones. If I handle it right, maybe the trogs won't spot you."

With a nod, Callan laid down at my feet. As I scooped loose stone up around her, she asked, "What are you going to do, David?"

"Once you're covered, I'll Boost and jump up on top of the boulders."

"Won't that put you in plain sight from the top of the hill?"

"If I planned on staying there, it would. I'm going to find a crevice or gap between boulders and slide down out of sight." I smoothed the rocks around Callan to appear more natural. Stroking her cheek once, I carefully piled stones around and over her head. "Stay as still as possible dear, don't say or do anything until I come for you, and remember that I'm nearby. I love you."

A muffled voice responded, "I love you, too, darling."

Upslope, I heard trogs moving closer so wasted no time issuing a command to my implant.

Boost!

Adrenaline flooded my veins and time slowed as strength surged through my body, driving away all my fatigue. I crouched and leapt up between two boulders. There were no handholds, so I simply pressed both arms against the sides of the two boulders. Boost-enhanced muscles locked against the rock, giving me the chance to swing the rest of my body up and over the top of the smaller boulder. Without Boost, my attempt would have been impossible. With Boost, I was over the top of the boulder and crouched in the crevice where two boulders met in a matter of seconds. Once I was safely out of sight, I dropped Boost.

I made it just in time. A few seconds after I dropped from sight

I heard several trogs stop at the top of the scree. A discussion of some kind followed, resulting in what I assumed was a call for the leader. The crunch of feet in loose stone announced the leader's arrival and I heard yet another discussion. The leader gave an order that resulted in what I could only interpret as a complaint. The leader spoke more harshly and the complainer shut up.

At long last, I heard many trog feet trudge away from the top of the scree and slowly fade away. Relieved, I started a slow count to thirty, planning to go pull Callan out at the end of the count. It's a good thing I waited. When my count reached nine I heard the unmistakable sound of two trogs climbing down the scree toward us.

With my heart hammering in my chest, I listened as the trogs slipped and slid down the stony slope toward the hidden body of their dead companion and my very living wife, also hidden beneath carefully piled stones. When I was certain the trogs were too far down the scree to spot me on top of the boulders, I crept up out of the crevice I'd hidden in and quietly drew my sword. I breathed through my mouth to reduce the already slim chance an exhalation might give away my presence. There was nothing I could do about the hammering of my heart.

I strained my ears, listening for the slightest change in the sounds made by the trogs. When the scrape of trogs sliding through rocks changed, it was so obvious a deaf man could have heard it. One second I heard two trogs noisily sliding and climbing and the next second the sound cut neatly in half. Either one of the trogs reached the bottom already—something I strongly doubted—or one of them slid into the corpse near the bottom of the scree.

A few seconds later, one of the trogs grunted in surprise and called to his companion. The call definitely didn't come from the bottom of the slope, meaning the trog had found the dead guard. My mind raced ahead, planning my response depending on what the trogs did next.

I fervently hoped they would simply climb back up the slope and go report to their leader. Callan and I could use that time to get out of the scree and find a better hiding place. I feared most that they'd yell for help, forcing me to attack and pray I not only killed the trogs quickly but could just as quickly find a better hiding place for Callan and me. Of course, the trogs didn't do either one of those things.

I listened to the trogs talk for a few seconds, my body tensed and ready to spring to the attack if either of them raised their voice. I heard the unmistakable sound of a trog climbing the rest of the way down the scree, joining the other trog at the bottom. Then I heard a spear plunge into the stones piled at the bottom of the scree and that made no sense to me.

Surely the trogs didn't think the person who killed the guard was also hiding down here? Okay, I *was* hiding down here, but there was no logical reason for the trogs to suspect that—especially since they'd already shot Chris running from this area. Their actions made no sense.

No, that's wrong. Poking spears into the rocks at the bottom of the scree made no sense based on *my* knowledge. So what did the trogs know that I didn't know? Lots of stuff and none of it was important at the moment. One of the trogs was directly below my boulder and mere feet from discovering Callan!

My tensed muscles uncoiled and I sprang from my boulder. I saw the trog below me jab his spear into stones piled against the boulder. Some sense warned the trog trouble was near because he looked up just in time to see me dropping toward him. His mouth opened to shout and he tried to raise his spear in defense. With the spear stuck a foot deep in the stones that was never going to work. Before he said anything, I rammed my sword through his right eye and out at the base of his skull.

The trog collapsed beneath me as I pulled my sword free. The other trog whirled at the sound of his companion hitting the ground. The trog's eyes widened at the sight, but his surprise didn't slow his reactions. With his own spear plunged into piled stones, the trog abandoned it and grabbed for the blaster rifle slung over his shoulder. The barrel of the dying trog's blaster stuck out from underneath his body. I'd never free that rifle fast enough to shoot first, but the other trog was too far away for me to reach before he fired.

I grabbed the trog's spear with my left hand and dove to my right. The spear pulled free easily and I readied it for an off-hand throw as I rolled to my feet. The trog swung the blaster rifle my way as I hurled the spear. It was a surprisingly accurate throw for a right-hander, flying arrow-straight toward the trog's chest. It was not a particularly hard throw and the trog deflected it easily with the blaster rifle. But that was my plan all along.

In the brief time the trog spent concentrating on the spear, I charged. While the spear clattered harmlessly off the rifle barrel, my sword thrust came up under his breast and skewered his heart. The trog stumbled backward, blue blood bubbling up out of his mouth and flowing freely down my sword blade. I pulled my sword free and, as if the blade was all that held him up, the trog collapsed.

I heard a sound behind me and spun, my sword held ready. A dirty and dust-covered Callan yanked at the barrel of the other trog's blaster rifle, struggling to pull it out from under the trog's body.

"It's okay, Callan, I got them both."

"I can see that, darling," she replied, wiggling the blaster to work it free. "But how long have we got before someone else comes looking for these two?"

I snatched up the blaster at my feet and ran to help Callan. "That's exactly the sort of question I should have thought of."

"Don't be so hard on yourself, David. You were rather busy."

I rolled the trog up and off of the blaster rifle, releasing the body once Callan pulled the weapon free. "Okay, let's climb out of here and see if we can find a place to hole up until the trogs stop looking for us."

Callan looked up at the boulder I'd leapt from. "There's no way out of here over the boulders?"

"Maybe, after a lot of dangerous hopping from boulder to

boulder we might find a way to safety. We might also find ourselves having to double back and climb this scree after all. But we can try-"

I interrupted myself as a new sound reached our ears. The droning of propellers told us an airship approached.

THE DOWNED AIRSHIP

Jade

Since our airship would be sailing north, the Oshwindon
Merchant Guild asked Dad to follow the approximate
course the *Sorrin* and the other two missing trade ships
followed. The guild mentioned, in the vaguest of terms, a reward
for information concerning the missing ships. I'd spent the
previous two days convincing him to do just what the council
asked, so he allowed the guild to talk him into doing what he was
already going to do. The guild even paid passage so one of their
senior members and his wife could accompany us.

If Dad knew the guild would send Vass Sune, I think he would
have refused their request. We'd still have searched for the missing
ships, but we would have done it without the company of the
Sunes. If there is a more odious couple in all of Oshwindon, I've
never heard of them. Despite that, Mr. Sune wielded a lot of power
in the guild and could make life very difficult for us if he
wanted to.

Dad had the whole family line up to welcome the Sunes aboard
our ship, the *Wind Dancer*. All three of us kids were bathed,
dressed in clean clothes, and unfailingly polite as Dad introduced
us.

Sasha smiled brightly and said, "I'm pleased to meet you."

Mrs. Sune tutted, "A properly brought-up girl would curtsey."

As Mom pulled Sasha close to her, Dad kept a stiff smile plastered on his face and introduced Will. My brother bowed over Mrs. Sune's hand to kiss it. I thought that was quite courageous of Will, since I was pretty sure Mrs. Sune's flesh was rotten.

Mrs. Sune jerked her hand away, crying, "Such impertinence! Really, Mrs. Cochran, did you even *try* teaching manners to your children?"

Mom glared daggers at the woman's back and pulled Will close, too. Mrs. Sune listened as Dad introduced me, but I knew he was wasting his time. Mrs. Sune radiated absolute disapproval as she gazed at me. I knew my next actions would prove futile, but I refused to let Mom and Dad down.

I curtseyed, though the effect was somewhat lost because I wasn't wearing a dress, and said, "Mr. and Mrs. Sune, we are honored to have you both aboard the *Wind Dancer*. If there is anything we can do to make your journey more enjoyable, please do not hesitate to ask."

I managed all of that without gagging and was pretty sure I even sounded sincere. Dad must have agreed, as he gave me a quick thumbs up.

Mrs. Sune sniffed and looked down her nose at me. "You *are* a girl, are you not?"

I imagined kicking the woman in the shin, that made it easier to keep a somewhat genuine smile on my face. "I am, Mrs. Sune."

Mrs. Sune humphed. She had to have set some kind of record for disapproving sounds, managing to tut, cry, sniff, and humph in the span of thirty seconds. But the woman wasn't finished with her performance.

"Tsk," she said, undoubtedly giving her the record—and all in less than forty seconds. "If you're a girl, why are you wearing boy's clothing?"

"A dress, while quite lovely, is inappropriate clothing for working aloft, ma'am," I said. This time I kept my smile by imagining the Sunes turning around and leaving the *Dancer*.

Mrs. Sune turned a glare on Dad but spoke to her husband. "Vass, why are we aboard a ship that lets this...child...take a role in keeping us safely flying?"

This time, Dad's smile slipped, but he kept his voice level. "Jade grew up on airships, Mrs. Sune. Despite her age, she is a very capable member of the crew."

Mrs. Sune returned to sniffing, ending her record run. "It is still quite inappropriate behavior for a girl."

Dad ignored the comment. Motioning to one of the crew to get the Sunes' baggage, he said, "I'll show you to your cabin."

That was just our first dealing with the lovely Mrs. Sune. Nothing about the the voyage pleased her.

The food was too hot.

The food was too cold.

The food was too spicy.

The food was too bland.

The tea was too weak.

The tea was too strong.

Her cabin was too small.

The ship flew too high.

Sasha was too energetic for a proper young girl.

Will was too mischievous for a proper young boy.

I was too...oh, take your pick, since absolutely *nothing* I did met her standards.

She even complained that she had difficulty walking when the wind was blowing. Geez, was Dad supposed to control the weather for her?

Through it all, Mom and Dad just listened politely and didn't grit their teeth or mutter under their breath until they were as far away from the woman as possible. Worse, the rest of us had to do the same thing. At least, I understood the politics of the situation and knew how much trouble the Sunes could cause for Dad if they chose to. Poor Will and Sasha just knew they had to be nice to the Sunes, even if the Sunes weren't nice to them in return.

Thank God I got to go aloft every now and then to take

lookout duty. I've always loved being on top of the envelope with just the wind and world to keep me company. With the Sunes down below, I would have bunked up there if Dad would have let me. Dad did agree that I should stay out of Mrs. Sune's sight as much as possible, so I got a *lot* of lookout duty. That meant I was the one who spotted the wreck.

"Downed airship four points to port! Twenty miles distance," I called through the speaking tube. "Look for the wisps of smoke rising from near it."

"We spy the smoke," Dad replied. "Can you identify the ship? Is it one of the missing merchant airships?"

She was keel-up on the desert floor and badly broken up. I studied the ship, mentally reconstructing her in the hope I could identify her. She was far too big for one of the merchant ships, that was certain. And then all of the pieces just sort of fell into place.

"She's not a merchant ship at all," I said. "She's...She looks like a Mordanian ship-of-the-line, Dad."

Dad was silent for a long time, then said, "I'm sending replacements up there. Then I want you to come down here, Jade."

"What? Come on, Dad, I can—"

"That's an order, Jade."

I sighed. There was only one possible response when Dad said that. "Aye aye, sir."

When I reached the deck, at least he let me watch as we drew nearer the wreck. Eight miles out, the new lookout called, "I found the source of the smoke, sir. It's...Uh, it's a big pile of burning bodies."

Dad look truly confused at the pronouncement and muttered, "What the hell does that mean?"

For once, I actually knew the answer. "I think I know, Dad."

He raised an eyebrow, his way of asking for an explanation.

"Trogs burn the bodies of their dead and those of honored foes." Dad's second eyebrow rose to join the first, so I added, "It says that in *David Rice and the City of the Trogs*. But it's also in some of the other books about his adventures."

Dad smiled. "It appears your insatiable appetite for all things David Rice has finally paid off in real life. Now, I want you to take your brother and sister below deck and stay there until I call for you."

"Dad, can't someone else watch Will and Sasha? I want to be up here if we run into trogs."

"And I want you below deck and safe for the very same reason." He gave me a hard look. "Do I have to make it an order?"

I hung my head. "No, sir."

That's how I missed my first chance to see real, live trogs.

NEW ALLIES

David

I caught Callan's hand and pulled her toward the scree. "We've got to get out of this deathtrap before the airship attracts the trogs!"

Sticking to the side of the scree, I used one hand to pull myself up, grabbing handholds on the rocks lining the edge of the slope. I used the other hand to pull Callan up behind me. We made surprisingly good time, all things considered, and this method allowed me to concentrate on climbing while Callan served as a lookout.

"Can you see the airship yet?" I asked between pants and gasps as I strained to get up the slope as fast as possible.

"Not yet. I think it's on the other side of this mountain." Callan was breathing nearly as hard as I was even though I was climbing for both of us. We had both been far too active with far too little rest. "Let's hope it stays there, too. If it swings around to our side of the mountain, it's bound to draw the trogs along with it."

Surely the crew would spot at least one of our wrecked airships and swoop down for a look. That, alone, ought to keep them busy for longer than it would take Callan and me to climb this slope.

Unless, my mind handily reminded me, they'd already investigated the wreck and were searching for survivors.

We passed the halfway point in our climb and I found myself wondering how the trogs would react to the airship. With blaster rifles, they could very well blast the ship out of the sky if it came within reasonable shooting range. Would the trogs fire on the ship or just hide and wait for it to sail away? Then I remembered the wind storm from the night before. Whoever was in charge of this place was pretty keen on keeping it a secret for as long as possible.

"The airship is slowing, David, and I think it will come around the mountain very soon."

"Almost to the top, dear."

"You'd better hurry, darling. The airship just flew into view." Callan was silent for a couple of seconds then spoke again. "And now the trogs are on the move. I can hear them walking on the loose stones."

"Can you get the attention of someone on the airship? A rain of crossbow bolts on the trogs will come in very handy if the trogs spot us."

I felt Callan stand up and her left arm began shaking a bit. I didn't have to look to know she was waving her right arm frantically, hoping someone on the airship spotted her.

"I just saw light reflect off of glass! Someone must be checking us out with binoculars." Callan waved even more frantically. "Yes! Someone waved back at me!"

"Good. Try pointing in the direction of the trogs. Even if they don't spot them, the captain should understand that there's danger nearby."

I hauled myself up to the top of the scree, pulling Callan up beside me. The sound of trogs walking through stone was much too loud for my tastes. I headed away from the approaching trogs, pulling Callan along with me. With a steep, bare slope rising above our little path and a rocky wasteland falling away below it, I didn't hold much hope of finding a hiding place.

"David, someone on the airship is pointing at the top of the mountain and motioning up. I think they want us to climb to the top so they can pick us up!"

Praying the trogs never chose to look our way, I left the path and led Callan up the wide open slope. I could feel her flagging as hunger and thirst and exhaustion took their toll. There was no way she could make the two hundred yard climb to the mountain top.

I took a look over my shoulder and saw the first trogs march into view. In the distance, the airship swung around for a pass over the mountain top. I thought I saw crossbowmen lining the rails before the airship turned bow forward to me. The ship's engines roared as the captain put on more speed. At the same time, a trog fired a very poorly aimed blaster shot. It missed the airship by a wide margin, but it served notice that the trogs weren't planning to let the airship get away.

Worst of all, I realized Callan and I had no chance of reaching the summit before the airship got there. There was only one thing to do. I turned and swept Callan into my arms. "Hang on, dear!"

Boost!

Adrenaline surged through my veins and time slowed. Callan wrapped her arms around my neck in slow motion as her expression gradually shifted from exhaustion to concern for me. I charged up the mountainside, my legs churning faster than any normal man's could. Then again, we Scouts aren't normal men—science and technology have seen to that.

I took another glance over my shoulder at the approaching airship. More blaster bolts blazed into the sky, but it looked like the trogs hadn't worked out the idea of aiming ahead of a moving target. Most of the bolts passed through the airship's wake and the rest missed to port or starboard. A volley of crossbow bolts launched from the airship, arching down toward the trogs. I couldn't see if any hit, but the trog shooting stopped and trog voices rose in alarm.

Then the bow of the airship passed over us. Men peered down at us waving arms and urging us to climb just a bit higher. Ropes dangled from the ship's railing, still too high for me to grab.

Knowing Callan would kill me if she realized what I was doing, I toggled off my implant's safety overrides. I swung Callan up over one shoulder as more adrenaline hit my system. I gave one final burst of speed and, just as the last rope passed overhead, I reached the mountaintop and leapt for the dangling line.

My fingers wrapped around the rope and strong arms pulled us to the safety of the deck. I carefully put Callan down then toggled on the implant safety overrides. The flow of adrenaline cut off and, for the first time since I'd originally arrived on Aashla, I fell unconscious before I even hit the deck.

Years ago, before the children were born, I frequently found myself forced to fight for Callan and country. I Boosted far too often and for far too long and rarely gave my body time to recover between Boosts. In retaliation, my body sometimes knocked me out to force inactivity on me. What can I say, sometimes my body knows what I need more than I do. I hadn't Boosted since I'd led the fight against pirate Captain Quint and his band of cutthroats, so the immunity I'd built up to the aftereffects of Boost was long gone.

In other words, my body planned on keeping me out for hours. For some perverse reason, life rarely cooperates in these situations. I found myself rising through gradually lightening shades of black until my eyes fluttered open, squinting into the bright desert sky. Cold water dribbled down my cheeks. Callan's face, wiped clean of dust and dirt and wearing a troubled look, hovered over me, a wooden cup in her hand. Looming above both of us stood two men, both gazing down at me with concern written on their faces.

"He's coming around." Callan put the cup down on the deck.

I raised a hand to wipe water from my eyes, got a look at my filthy fingers, and decided better of it. "We must be in serious trouble for *you* to wake me up after I pushed my Boosting limits."

"Aye, that we are," one of the looming men said. "There's...

something...in our wake and it's moving right quick, too. Her Highness agreed we need your opinion."

"You know who we are?"

"Only a blind man could fail to recognize Princess Callan—even covered in dust," the man replied. "And who but her husband could run faster *up* a mountain—while carrying his wife, no less—than any normal, unburdened man could run down the same mountain?"

Suppressing a groan, I sat up. "I'm sorry I missed the introductions. And you'd be?"

The man raised a hand in half-salute. "Lon Cochran, owner and captain of the *Wind Dancer*." Smiling briefly at my raised eyebrow, Cochran offered a hand to help me stand. "My oldest daughter chose the name and proud I was to register it."

"As I would have been in your place. I have a daughter, too." I arched my back and stretched. "Now where is this strange pursuer?"

Cochran led me to the stern, handed me a pair of Federation-made binoculars, and pointed at a dot off in the distance. I raised the binoculars and swept the area until I found the object. With the touch of a button, I zoomed in for a closer view and gasped.

"It sort of looks like a normal airship, 'cept I've got no idea how it flies without an envelope," Cochran said.

"Proscribed galactic tech is how, Captain." I increased the magnification slowly, careful to keep the distant airship centered in my view. "Can this ship go any faster?"

"Mister Yarrow," Cochran's voice took on the edge of command, "raider drill."

"Aye, Captain!" The other man who had loomed above me turned away from us, snapping off orders to the crew.

"What's raider drill, Captain?" Callan asked.

"We dump the cargo and bring up the boiler pressure on the ship's pinnace. If raiders get too close, my family and our passengers can escape in the pinnace while the crew and I stay and fight."

"I'd advise putting your family aboard the pinnace as soon as possible. Without the drag of an envelope slowing it down, I don't see how we can outrun that airship." I continued examining the approaching airship. Beyond the blaster rifles carried by the entirely human crew, I saw no signs of any advanced weaponry. "Have you got a good pilot to fly the pinnace?"

"Aye, Captain Rice. Jade, the same daughter who named the *Dancer*."

"Good." I lowered the binoculars. "Callan, you—"

"Will go on the pinnace. Yes, darling."

My eyebrows rose almost to my hairline. "Who are you and what have you done with my wife?"

"Perhaps motherhood has changed my perspective. Besides, *someone* has to remain free to organize the rescue."

"And who better to do that than Lady Death herself?"

Callan rolled her eyes and turned toward Cochran. "You wouldn't be in this danger had you not come looking for survivors from our wrecks, Captain. The Mordanian treasury will reimburse you for your losses."

"What say we worry about that after we're all safe, Your Highness?"

Before Callan could reply, a tall blonde girl of fifteen or sixteen years crowded in between Callan and Cochran. "Yarrow says you're sending me off in the pinnace, Dad."

"*Mister* Yarrow. And yes, I need you to pilot it away from that thing." Cochran waved a hand toward the distant airship.

The girl turned bright green eyes on our pursuer and stared for a few seconds. "How the hell does it fly?"

"Watch your tongue, Jade!" Cochran shook his head in dismay. "We have visitors."

Apparently noticing us for the first time, Cochran's daughter gave us a dismissive glance. Then her eyes widened and swung back to us—alighting on me for some reason. Her mouth formed an 'O' of surprise.

"Oh my God! You're *him*!"

I smiled and sketched a brief bow. "David Rice at your service, Miss Cochran. And may I present my wife, Princess Callan?"

Jade's eyes cut to Callan for a split second. "Hi." Then the girl's eyes snapped back to me and she just stared.

"Jade, get busy preparing the pinnace," her father ordered. His daughter didn't move or speak or show that she'd heard a thing her father said. Cochran caught Jade's jaw and gently turned her to face him. "I *said* go prepare the pinnace for launch. You're taking Princess Callan along with your mother, Will, Sasha, and the Sunes."

"Oh, right! Um, aye aye, Dad." Jade turned away but managed to keep her eyes on me until the last second.

Cochran sighed as she scampered aft. "My apologies to you both. The girl has much better manners than that but, well..."

"She has the good taste to be smitten with David," Callan finished for Cochran.

Cochran nodded. "He was her first big crush. She's read all of the books and has even got one of those photo graph things of him pinned to the bulkhead in her cabin."

Before I could come up with a response to that news, the first boxes of cargo crashed into the ground hundreds of feet beneath the *Wind Dancer*. Knowing time was short, I pulled Callan close for a quick kiss.

"Take care of yourself, darling," she whispered into my ear.

"I will. You do the same."

Two minutes later, the pinnace launched from the *Dancer's* bow and slowly pulled away from the larger, heavier ship. Then I returned to the bow and once again focused on the approaching airship. It was still well astern of us but close enough for me to make out individual faces—and one of them was all too familiar.

Raoul, exiled prince of Tarteg, captained the pursuing airship.

I just stared through the binoculars for a few seconds wondering exactly what terrible sins I had committed in a previous life. Why else would God see fit to counter the boundless joy my family gives me with a pathetic, revenge-minded festering wound of a human like Raoul? And what kind of idiot would turn such a man loose on Aashla with galactic tech?

I lowered the binoculars. "Well, hell."

"You look like you swallowed a live hornet, Captain Rice," Cochran said. "What did you see?"

"The captain of our pursuing airship. He's none other than my arch pain in the ass, Raoul." I sighed, handing the binoculars back to Cochran. "He and I have crossed paths several times though not in the last five or six years."

"And Raoul always comes out the worse for being foolish enough to go up against you." Cochran grinned at the surprised look I gave him. "Even if Jade hadn't told us all about your adventures dozens of times, we'd know about you and Raoul. I expect most everyone on Aashla does by now. That's likely to make Raoul hate you even more, of course."

"Count on it." I glanced over my shoulder at the pinnace that was now well ahead of us. "On the plus side, once Raoul spots me he will completely ignore the pinnace."

"Let's not waste any time waiting for him to notice." Cochran called his signal man over. "Mister Gant, could you please send a message to the airship behind us? Tell them Captain David Rice is aboard and warn them to turn back before he gets angry."

As Gant climbed to his signal perch, I couldn't help but grin. "That message will have Raoul seeing red!"

Gant was only halfway through the message when the first crewman fired at us. A few more shots flashed our way, none of them coming remotely close to hitting the *Wind Dancer*, before someone—probably Raoul, who no doubt wanted to watch me die up close and personal—got the crew under control again.

"Veer away from the pinnace's course, Captain Cochran," I said. "We need to make sure Raoul follows us rather than our families."

Cochran ordered a sweeping course change to due north. To our considerable relief, the anti-grav airship followed us. Indeed, Raoul performed a more abrupt course change, cutting inside the arc of our turn and slicing off a big chunk of our lead in the process.

Shortly after that, another blaster bolt flew our way, missing the *Dancer* by a good ten yards. My hopes for a fusillade of poorly aimed shots that did nothing but drain power packs failed to materialize. Instead, one crewman fired every thirty seconds.

"Ranging shots," Cochran said. "Smart move on their part and a much more disciplined approach than I expected. Once they get in range, those rifles could wipe us all out before the airship comes within crossbow range."

"I know. I had three of the rifles in my hands before I made my mad dash to catch a ride with you. I had to drop them to carry Callan."

"I don't think three rifles would make much difference, David."

"Especially *those* three rifles. The trogs never cleaned them. They had so much dirt and grit in them-"

Cochran raised an eyebrow when I stopped speaking. "Problem?"

"No, solution. Maybe." I leaned over the railing and looked at the ground five hundred feet below us. It was just what I hoped for. "Do you trust your pilot to fly this fast but at an altitude of twenty feet?"

"Why?"

"The inner workings of those blaster rifles are open to the air, so it's easy for dirt to get into it. If enough gunk gets into those rifles, they should stop working."

"So you want to use the *Dancer's* engines to kick dirt in Raoul's face and into his rifles as well." Cochran nodded as if the idea appealed to him. "Let's give it a try!"

Over the next minute and a half, the *Wind Dancer* descended steadily. Once Raoul figured out what we were doing, he dropped steadily, keeping us within range of the blaster rifles. By the time we leveled off, our engines kicked up a brown cloud of dirt and dust and sand in our wake. The fine particles served a second purpose, absorbing and dissipating the blaster bolts' energy, essentially forming an energy shield between us and Raoul's airship.

Raoul stuck to our stern, though he never descended far enough to match our altitude. The fringes of the dust cloud still enveloped his ship, giving us hope the blaster rifles were fouling. Raoul also kept shooting at us every thirty seconds, gauging a blaster bolt's range through the dust cloud. Captain Cochran returned the favor with crossbows when the other airship pulled within fifty yards of us. To my delight, crossbow bolts flew far better through the dust than blaster bolts did. When our crossbowman winged Raoul's rifleman, Raoul ascended out of crossbow range and, unfortunately, out of the dust cloud.

"Is Raoul giving up?" Cochran asked me when the *Dancer's* envelope blocked our view of the other airship.

"Not likely. I'll climb up on top of the envelope and see what he's up to."

"The hell you will!" Cochran's expression brooked no argument. "I will not be the man who loses Aashla's greatest hero to a random gust of wind."

With a few shouted commands, two of Cochran's crew ran up into the airship's rigging and up the side of the envelope. Seconds later, the two men descended even faster than they went up.

"The other ship's coming down on top of us!" shouted one.

"Brace for impact!" cried the second.

Then the airship shuddered as a great weight dropped onto the envelope and drove the ship toward the ground. Timber snapped and splintered as the *Wind Dancer* crashed bow-first into the ground.

CHANGING FLAGS

Callan

C aptain Cochran's young son offered me a hand up into the little pinnace. I didn't need the assistance, but smiled gratefully and accepted the boy's hand.

"Thank you, Master Cochran."

The lad's eyes gleamed as he responded in a formal tone, "You're most welcome, Your Highness. I'd be most pleased if you would call me Will."

I settled into a seat on the pinnace as the rest of the passengers came up on deck and were helped aboard. Besides Captain Cochran's wife and youngest daughter—an energetic girl of about six named Sasha—there was a gaunt man in his middle years and his plump wife.

Our pilot, Jade, bounded onto the pinnace and went straight to the controls. After a quick scan of the dials, she turned to the crewmen holding the pinnace at bay. "Release the lines!"

The little airship rose from the deck as Jade fed power to the propellers. Taking off from a moving airship is trickier than most people know. Without careful control on the part of the pilot, the pinnace's propeller could slice through crewmen, the lines connecting the parent ship's hull and the envelope, or even the envelope itself. Jade's eyes never stopped moving as she deftly maneuvered the pinnace away from the *Wind Dancer*.

"What is the meaning of this?" The plump wife turned a glare on her gaunt husband. "Vass, why don't we have a *real* pilot for this airship?"

Prompted by his wife, the man turned his own glare on Mrs. Cochran. "I would like an answer to that question, myself. The very idea of trusting our lives to a mere girl! Rest assured, Mrs. Cochran, I will register a most stern protest with the merchant guild."

I inherited my mother's short temper, which I struggle to hold in check for the sake of court diplomacy. But this pinnace was far from the Mordanian Court, so I relished one of my rare chances to release my temper. "That *girl* is handling a very difficult bit of piloting and doing it exceedingly well. Now kindly be silent and stop distracting Jade from her job!"

The couple turned their glares on me but kept quiet. Mrs. Cochran smiled gratefully at me, as did young Will. Jade never changed expression or even gave an indication she heard the exchange. Thirty seconds later, the pinnace pulled away from the *Wind Dancer* and Jade relaxed a bit.

The plump wife wasted no time venting her anger at me. "How dare you take such a tone with me, young woman! Do you have any idea who my husband is?"

Putting my elbows on the pinnace's railing, I leaned back nonchalantly. "I neither know nor care who your husband is, madam. Do you know who *I* am?"

Vass, the gaunt husband, sniffed. "A well-mannered young woman, which you most assuredly are not, would show respect to her elders and introduce herself first."

Captain Cochran told David a man would have to be blind not to recognize me. Since neither of these two was blind, I had to assume their heads were stuck too far up their backsides to see me clearly. I turned on what David calls my princess glare and was pleased to see the couple pull back slightly.

"I usually have someone with me to handle introductions, but he stayed behind on the *Wind Dancer* to ensure that we all got safely away."

I felt a tug at my sleeve from Will. "May I introduce you, please?"

I sat up and inclined my head. "It is most kind of you to offer, Will. I would be honored if you would proffer introductions."

The boy stood and bowed slightly to the irritating couple. "This is Mr. Vass Sune, merchant of the city-state of Oshwindon, and Mrs. Sune, his wife. Sir and madam, may I make known to you Her Royal Highness, Princess Callan, heir to the throne of Mordan."

Rob, the much-missed late captain of my guard and namesake to my son, taught me many things during his years of service. Among those lessons was to never take pleasure in the discomfort of others. I guess that's one lesson that just didn't stick, because I took considerable pleasure watching the Sunes' mouths open and close without any sound emerging. They looked exactly like a couple of fish out of water—or at least out of their depth.

Ignoring them, I smiled at Will. "That was very well done. Where did you learn all of that?"

Will flushed with pleasure but wasn't inclined to answer. Mrs. Cochran answered for him. "Jade has all of the adventures they've written about your husband and reads them aloud to Will and Sasha. I don't doubt my son can recite most of the stories word-for-word, he's heard them so often. I'm sure he learned those words in the stories."

Behind us, the *Wind Dancer* gracefully changed course, swinging out of our wake and onto a northerly heading. Without the massive envelope above it, Raoul's distant airship was more difficult to see. Then the dot elongated, evidence it was also changing course to follow the *Wind Dancer*.

The Sunes finally found their voices and offered profuse apologies. I waved off the whole affair before heading aft to put some distance between the Sunes and me and to watch the *Wind Dancer* for as long as possible.

"Thank you for defending me, Your Highness," Jade said quietly.

"Your piloting skill should be all the defense required," I replied. "I did nothing but point it out."

Behind us, Mrs. Sune spoke in a stage whisper, apparently thinking me too far away to hear her. "Mrs. Cochran, why did you not tell us you had royalty on board your airship? It is your fault we made such a poor initial impression on Her Highness!"

"They only came aboard twenty minutes before we left on the pinnace, Mrs. Sune. No slight was intended," Mrs. Cochran replied quietly and far more politely than the Sune woman deserved.

I turned back toward the Sunes, preparing to unleash my temper yet again. Jade caught my eye and shook her head. "I know you wish to help, Your Highness, but please don't."

"Why is your mother so polite to those people? And what are you afraid will happen if I speak up?"

"The *Wind Dancer* is registered in Oshwindon and flies their flag." Repressed anger smoldered behind Jade's green eyes. "Mr. Sune is a powerful member of the city-state's merchant guild. He can cause real trouble for us if he wants to."

I considered the problem for all of one second. "Could they bother you if the *Wind Dancer* was a Mordanian-flagged trading vessel?"

Jade snorted. "No, Your Highness. The Oshwindon merchant guild needs Mordan more than Mordan needs the merchant guild. But you, of all people, must know the large fees required to register as a Mordanian vessel. And there's a long waiting list, too."

"You do realize your father saved my life when he pulled David and me off that mountain, don't you? My family takes our debts seriously." I switched to my princess-of-the-realm voice. "On behalf of your father, will you accept my royal decree naming the *Wind Dancer* and any other ships your family owns, now and in the future, Mordanian-flagged trading vessels?"

"You can do that?" Jade goggled at me. "I mean, you can do that, Your Highness?"

"Does that mean yes, Jade?"

The pretty young woman nodded emphatically. I turned my attention back to the ongoing recriminations Mrs. Sune threw at Mrs. Cochran, who remained polite and deferential throughout the harangue. "Mrs. Cochran, may I be the first to welcome you and your family to the Mordanian merchant fleet?"

All eyes turned my way as a startled Mrs. Cochran said, "Pardon me, Your Highness, I must have misheard you."

"You heard just fine, Mrs. Cochran. By royal decree, your family now sails under the Mordanian flag. These people," I pointed at the Sunes, "no longer hold any power over you. Please feel free to stop deferring to this woman's craven attempts to lay her boorish behavior at your feet."

Mrs. Cochran stared at me for a few brief seconds. "Thank you, Your Highness! Oh my, you have no idea what this means to us!"

"I owe your family my life." I turned back to the Sunes, igniting my princess glare again. "If I hear the barest whisper that you have used your position in Oshwindon to cause even the slightest trouble to the Cochrans, I will personally see to it that my father enacts a special tariff on all goods offloaded by Oshwindon airships. We'll call it the Sune Surtax. I'm sure it will make you quite popular among the other Oshwindon merchants."

"W-w-why we would never *dream* of causing problems for these fine folk, Your Highness!" Mr. Sune stammered.

"Your Highness!" The urgency in Jade's voice drove the Sunes from my mind.

Spinning around, I saw Jade pointing toward the *Wind Dancer.* More accurately, I saw her pointing to where the *Wind Dancer* used to be. A billowing cloud of dust hid both the *Dancer* and Raoul's airship from sight.

"What does the cloud of dust mean?" Jade asked.

"It means we can change course and hide from Raoul and his

crew." I scanned the horizon, looking for some feature besides the flat expanse of the desert and the sharp mountains where the galactics had their base of operations. "Do you see anything that can conceal this pinnace?"

"Now see here, Your Highness," Vass Sune protested, "Cochran sent us off in this airship so we could get away from those pursuers! Surely it is unwise to go against the good Captain's wishes."

"Well, I think it's f-," Jade gave her mother a sidelong glance. "It's, uh, brilliant."

"Mrs. Cochran, you have children aboard so the final decision rests in your hands," I said. "We may escape that airship if we continue our flight, but we might also simply prolong the inevitable."

The woman looked at her three children, then back at the cloud of dust, before turning to me. "What would you advise?"

"Fly away, obviously!" Mrs. Sune responded superciliously. "How can you even consider another action, you foolish woman?"

"Out of the mouths of harpies..." Jade muttered.

"That is truly invaluable advice, Mrs. Sune," Mrs. Cochran said, smiling sweetly at the merchant's wife. Turning back to me, Jade's mother added, "We shall find a place to hide."

The older woman spluttered, "What nonsense is this?"

Her husband added acerbically, "Is that meant as some type of jest? Why would you ignore advice you said was invaluable?"

"In the two weeks your wife has traveled with us, she has never failed to share her opinion on matters ranging from child rearing to food preparation to airship navigation. She has never let her complete lack of experience in any of these matters deter her." Mrs. Cochran's face grew stern. "Never have her opinions been even remotely useful. I would go so far as to say a woman could lead quite a successful life by asking Mrs. Sune's advice on all matters and doing the exact opposite. I'm testing that theory now."

The Sunes' compressed their lips in displeasure and, mercifully, fell silent. Will whooped and little Sasha clapped her hands.

Jade grinned. "Damn, Mom, that was patchless!"

Mrs. Cochran returned her daughter's grin. "Is that good?"

Jade rolled her eyes. "Yes, Mom. If clothes or a gas envelope don't have patches, that means they're perfect."

"Ah," her mother nodded. "I'd have said they were tightly stitched when I was your age."

Jade's eyebrows rose. "You had slang back in the olden days?"

"Of course we did, Jade. Your generation may have changed the words, but they didn't invent the concepts any more than my generation did." Mrs. Cochran flashed a downright wicked smile at her daughter. "Come to me after you're married, daughter, and I'll tell you about a lot of *other* things your generation didn't invent!"

I laughed, reminded of my own mother's advice on matters of love. Jade, on the other hand, blushed furiously and turned her attention to the horizon. A moment later, the girl's stare intensified and she pointed into the distance.

"Your Highness, there's a wreck a couple of miles away." Jade shielded her eyes from the sun. "Mom, I think it might be the *Sorrin*!"

I looked at Mrs. Cochran and raised an eyebrow.

"We flew this route partially to search for the *Sorrin*. It is—or at least it was—one of the fastest merchant airships flying under the Oshwindon flag. One of the younger crewmen has taken a fancy to Jade." The look on Mrs. Cochran's face spoke volumes concerning her low opinion of this young man. To her credit, when Jade's mother spoke next, her voice held obvious concern. "I do hope the boy is all right."

"Don't worry about Forbose, Mom." Jade was almost hopping with excitement. "He knows how to take care of himself!"

"Of *that* I have no doubt, dear." Mrs. Cochran's tone could have taught the desert a thing or two about dryness.

Jade's eyebrows drew down and I felt certain we were about to witness the resumption of an ongoing family disagreement. I jumped in with a question, hoping to divert attention back to our current problems. "Jade, how long will it take to deflate the envelope enough to hide in that wreck?"

Startled by the change of subject, Jade's simmering anger faded into calculation. "If we can anchor the pinnace, we won't have to deflate at all. We can just winch the envelope down until it's flush with the deck. We'll blend into the desert well enough that someone will have to be right on top of us to see us."

"Ah, is that why the envelope is the same color as the desert?" I asked, keeping Jade thinking about anything except arguing over her boyfriend.

"Yeah. I mean, yes Your Highness. It helps hide the pinnace if we have to abandon ship and run from raiders."

"We're nowhere near a formal court, Jade. You and your family may call me Callan. It's a lot easier on everyone and much faster in an emergency."

Jade looked at her mother who nodded. "If you say so, Callan."

"I say," Mr. Sune said, "if someone as important as you is missing, Callan, can we expect the Mordanian Navy to come to our rescue?"

"First, I gave Jade and her family leave to call me Callan. *You* have not been given such leave."

The Sunes' jaws dropped open. Of course, Mrs. Sune found her voice first. "You would put these…these…*people* above *us?*"

I flashed a vicious smile at the couple. "Why, yes, I would. As for a Naval rescue, I wouldn't count on anything for at least another day, probably more. Even then, it will probably be a Federation ship."

By then, Jade was piloting the pinnace in among the wreckage of the *Sorrin.* I pitched in with the Cochran family to fend the little airship off of jagged timbers jutting out of the broken hull. We anchored the pinnace to the largest piece of hull and carefully winched the envelope down to the deck. The sour expressions on the Sunes' faces when they discovered they had to debark lightened everyone else's mood considerably. Will and Jade tossed loose timbers on top of the envelope, further camouflaging our airship.

Thirty minutes after we finished, the sound of an airship's engine came to us. I carefully looked over the top of the wreck and my heart sank. The strange airship without an envelope was steaming our way.

A FINAL CONFESSION

David

Captain Cochran grabbed my arm and pulled me toward the stern railing. "Jump!"

All around the deck, crewman dove off the ship. As Cochran and I vaulted into open air I swore the ground was a lot more than twenty feet below us. We hung there for a second that lasted an hour and then plunged toward the ground. Behind us, the *Wind Dancer* continued its grinding disintegration against the hard-packed ground of the desert.

When I reached the ground, I did just as my trainers at the academy taught me to do. I hit with my knees bent to absorb some of the impact then let my entire body collapse into a momentum-draining roll. Pain lanced through my ankles, knees, and hips before the roll spread the hurt around to all parts of my body. When I finally rolled to a stop, I took quick stock of myself, flexing my legs and arms and twisting my neck. Everything ached but nothing was broken, so I struggled to my feet.

Cochran lay a few feet away, holding his leg and cursing. I knelt next to him and pulled his hands away from his leg. It was obviously broken.

"I'm not dying," Cochran said through gritted teeth. "Go check on my crew."

I rose to my feet, sketching a salute. "Aye aye, Captain!"

I'd love to recount how I sprinted to the wreck to look for survivors, but the truth is the best I could manage was a fast hobble. My ankles and knees screamed with every step I took so I ordered my implant to release painkillers into my system. Within seconds, my speed increased to a slow jog. I called out to crewmen as I passed them and found none in desperate need of assistance. Three of the crewmen were dead, but they had grief-stricken friends taking care of their bodies.

The wreck of the *Dancer* spread out from the impact point for well over one hundred yards, with timber scattered and piled all along its path. A few fires burned but, through some miracle, neither boiler exploded. Both had great holes in them from burst seams and the metal ticked and popped as it cooled. Moans and cries for help rose from half a dozen places and a few of the healthier crewmen were already helping free trapped men and move those too injured to move themselves.

As I surveyed the scene, deciding where I could be the most helpful, I heard a low thrumming from overhead. The anti-grav airship hovered above me. Half a dozen men trained blasters on me as Raoul smiled in triumph.

"Going somewhere, Rice?"

"Yes, Raoul, I'm going to help the crew of the airship you just wrecked."

"I wouldn't have wrecked them if they hadn't taunted me!"

"Yes, you would." I turned and resumed walking toward the nearest crewmen working to free a man buried under broken timber.

"Stop where you are or I'll order my men to shoot!"

If Raoul was going to shoot me, he'd have already done it. At least, I hoped that was the case. "Is this how you repay me for rescuing you in the tunnels under Beloren?"

"I could have escaped on my own!"

"Then why didn't you?" I reached the mound of debris and pulled a long, broken board from the pile. "Face it, Raoul, without

Martin and me you'd have been tammar food. Now please shut up so I can get on with my work."

The men and I worked for about a minute before I felt the prick of a sword in my back. I marveled that Raoul was stupid enough to abandon his superior position and superior firepower.

"Draw your sword and face me, Rice."

I stepped away from the crewmen and drew my sword. Turning around, I found Raoul in a classic dueling stance. Four of his men —all armed with blaster rifles—stood well back from him, keeping watch on the crew. The rifles looked dusty, but I was too far away to see if the inner workings were dust fouled.

Raoul slashed the air with his blade. "Let's go, Rice!"

Far be it from me to deny Raoul his duel.

Boost!

Adrenaline poured into my veins, time slowed, and my aches vanished. I flicked my blade at Raoul's wrist to disarm him, then I could put my sword to Raoul's throat and force his crew to surrender.

I was already stepping forward to grab Raoul when he parried my blade and sliced at my own wrist. Shocked, I barely pulled my arm back in time to avoid the thrust.

Raoul danced back lightly and he did *not* move in slow motion.

"Surprise, Rice," Raoul said. "You and Bane are no longer the only men on Aashla who can Boost!"

My eyes widened in surprise and I felt my concentration waver from the duel as the implications of Raoul's pronouncement hit me. If the exiled prince had shown the barest hint of patience and waited two seconds, I'd have dropped my guard entirely and been an easy target for the point of his blade. Instead, Raoul launched a furious attack and my mind snapped back to the task at hand.

One after another, I parried Raoul's attacks. I also fell back from his onslaught, unable to mount any kind of counterattack. Trained in the art of swordsmanship almost from birth, Raoul's skill easily surpasses mine with a blade. It's been almost a decade since the one time the two of us crossed blades on the deck of the

Pauline. Raoul had driven me back that time, too. But back then I'd been carefully drawing Raoul into a trap.

I deflected another attack, but Raoul's blade still scored a cut to my upper arm. Raoul grinned and stamped and wove his blade all around before me, leaving me wondering how such a dangerous swordsman could be so utterly unimaginative in everything else he did. A glimmer of hope followed on the heels of that thought. Raoul was quick, strong, and relentless with the sword, but he was also fixated entirely on me. Perhaps I could use that to turn the tables.

I recalled a small pile of debris from the wreck and carefully allowed Raoul to drive me backward to it. A grin split Raoul's face and grew wider with each retreating step I took toward the debris. No doubt visions of me tripping over the broken timbers played through Raoul's mind, surely followed by his sword driving through my heart. I fed those fantasies with widened eyes and rapid breathing. Raoul feinted at my shoulder then swept his blade around for a cut to my throat, all designed to force me to step back and trip over the debris. Against any normal man, the plan would have worked even if the opponent knew what was coming.

Because of Boost, I am not a normal man. As Raoul feinted, I launched myself into a backward flip that carried me over the pile of debris and safely to the other side. Expecting some kind of resistance to his attack, Raoul found his lunge unblocked and his forward momentum unchecked. With the choice of taking another step forward or falling on his face, Raoul took a hasty, off-balance step forward—right onto the pile of debris. The broken planks shifted under his weight and Raoul crashed to the ground at my feet.

I planted a foot in the small of Raoul's back and pressed my sword against his neck. "Yield or die, Raoul."

A calm, controlled voice speaking in galactic basic, said, "Release him, Mr. Rice, or I shall be forced to order my men to open fire on the crew of your ship."

Keeping my foot and sword in place, I turned toward the anti-grav airship. A man close to my own height, though probably twice my age, stood on the deck. He wore the everyday clothing of galactic society and an imperturbable expression on his face. It was the look of a man confident in himself and his place in the universe.

"Before making threats, whoever you are, I suggest you take a look at the inner workings of those rifles." Raoul stirred under my foot so I put more weight on it. "Dissipating your blaster shots was a benefit of our dust cloud, but that wasn't its primary objective."

A frown creased the man's face as he took a blaster rifle from a member of his crew. The frown deepened as he studied the weapon. "Very clever, Mr. Rice. It appears I've underestimated you. It won't happen again."

The man turned to the four crewmen on the ground and spoke in a language I didn't know, though it sounded like one of the southern city-state dialects. The four men abandoned their positions, grabbing ropes dropped to them from the deck of the airship. As the crew hauled them up to the deck, the thrum of the anti-grav increased. Swinging about, the airship rose into the sky and flew back the way we'd come.

"What the hell?"

The words came from my feet. I'd been so distracted by the galactic on the airship, I'd forgotten all about the former prince. I regarded the man at my feet and shook my head.

"You know Raoul, you can't pick allies worth a damn."

Raoul lay at my feet, disconsolately staring after the retreating airship. There was a time—long, long ago—when I had felt sympathy for Raoul and his cruel nickname of the Spare Prince. That was before I got to know him and learned what a back-stabbing, small-minded, revenge-driven jerk he was. When faced with a choice between right or wrong, truth or falsehood, courage or cowardice, I've never seen Raoul make the noble choice even one time. Inevitably, his poor choices proved disastrous for others. From Rob, Callan's lifelong guard, to the three dead crewmen from the *Wind Dancer*, someone else always paid the ultimate price for Raoul's stupidity.

I leaned all of my weight onto the foot on Raoul's back and stuck my sword half an inch into his shoulder. "I said yield or die."

My foot forced the breath out of Raoul. It mixed with a sharp cry of pain from my shoulder stab, resulting in a ridiculous squeak. Dropping his head onto the ground, Raoul tossed his sword away. "I yield."

I removed my foot from Raoul's back and waved my blade before his face. "Get up."

Raoul struggled to his feet, wincing at the pain from muscles overtaxed by Boost. "What are you going to do with me, Rice? You defeated me even when I could Boost, completely humiliating me in the process. What's left other than death?"

I pointed to the bodies of the *Dancer's* three dead crewmen, around which the surviving crew gathered. "Go over there."

Raoul stared at me for a few seconds, shrugged, and trudged in the direction I pointed. Two crewmen supported Captain Cochran, whose broken leg dangled untreated beneath him. His face screwed up in anguish, Cochran stared down at the bodies. Tears flowed down the Captain's cheeks and he shook his head from side to side as if refusing to recognize the bodies at his feet could bring them back to life.

Cochran looked down on a man about my own age. "How am I going to face Risha and her little boy and tell them Van is dead? Van's boy worshiped him." Cochran's gaze shifted to a young man of perhaps twenty years. "Poor Min is at home right now, happy as you please planning her wedding to Thom. And now there won't be a wedding or a life together." Finally, Cochran's eyes slid to the smallest body—a boy no more than fourteen. "And Charlie. God in heaven, I told his mother I'd look after him! How can I even look her in the face after this?"

"Do you see what you have done, Raoul?" I asked. "Not only have you killed three good men, you've devastated the lives of countless others who knew and loved those men!"

Every member of the crew turned our way when I spoke. Their distraught faces turned angry at the sight of Raoul. Fists bunched at their sides and a low growl ran through them.

His eyes locked on me, Raoul made an elaborate shrug and said, "Men die, Rice."

The crew's low growl rose to a roar and they surged at the exiled prince. True to form, Raoul realized his danger too late. He turned to face the onslaught and immediately Boosted.

With proper training and experience, one Boosted man can defeat a mob in hand-to-hand fighting. Raoul had neither training nor experience. He flailed about, landing lots of punches, but he didn't analyze the mob's movements. His dodges kept a few blows from landing, but he didn't lead his opponents into hitting each other rather than him. Without any tactics on Raoul's part, the crew soon swarmed over him and pinned his arms and legs. A big, strong crewman knelt on top of Raoul and mercilessly beat the prince's face to a pulp.

Angry as the crew was at Raoul, they weren't murderers. A minute or so after they swarmed over Raoul, the beating stopped and the crew just walked away. To my surprise, Raoul's eyes blinked open and he stared at me through bloody, swollen eyes. The idiot must have kept Boosting through the beating.

Shaking my head in disgust, I said, "Drop Boost and let yourself pass out, Raoul."

Spitting blood from his mouth, Raoul said, "I can't."

"What do you mean?"

"It won't turn off, Rice."

"The beating must have damaged it. See if you can find a way to shut down the whole implant!"

Raoul shook his head. "I didn't even turn Boost on. It just started when the crew attacked."

"You'll die from Boost Burnout if you can't turn it off!"

"I think that's what *he* wants."

"The galactic in the airship?"

Raoul nodded. "He doesn't want me telling you his secrets. So listen carefully, Rice. You won't have a second chance."

I ordered my implant to record Raoul's words. "Go. Speak as fast as you can."

For the next six minutes, Raoul told me everything he could about the two rogue galactics and their plans. With each passing minute, the prince's body grew tauter and his face more drawn. By the final minute, his words came in gasps as he struggled against his body to tell me everything I needed to combat the menace and, in Raoul's mind, take revenge for his death.

In mid-word, Raoul's body arched and blood gushed from his mouth as his heart finally burst under the stress of Boost. I closed Raoul's eyes and searched for some sense of sorrow, some depth of feeling for the man's death. I felt nothing beyond a sense of relief that Raoul would never endanger me or mine again.

I went to Captain Cochran. Assured by the *Dancer's* medic that he had tended all of the serious crew injuries, Cochran sat still while the man splinted his Captain's broken leg. I got to Cochran just in time to help set his leg, helping a second crewman hold the Captain down during the procedure. Cochran sucked breath through gritted teeth when the medic aligned the bones then turned his pale face my way.

"The Spare Prince is dead?"

"Yes."

"Good." Cochran laid his head back on the ground. "He went quickly. Did he suffer?"

"More than you can possibly imagine. I've come close to Boost Burnout once and Raoul's last few minutes were...unpleasant."

"God have mercy on my soul, but I am not sorry to hear that."

"Many others will feel as you do when they hear of Raoul's death. His brother Rupor, who still remembers Raoul before court intrigue changed him, may be the only man who will truly mourn Raoul's death."

"Family is like that—using the good memories to paper over the bad," Cochran said. "But what did Raoul tell you during his last minutes? Did you learn anything useful we can use against these two galactics?"

"Quite a bit, actually, though there's no 'we' in this." Cochran tried to rise and I gently pushed him back down. "You have a broken leg and half of your crew is injured. You'll need the uninjured half to take care of you until rescue arrives. Besides, I can move more quickly by myself."

"We're miles from the...base? Lair? Whatever you want to call where these galactics are hiding. It'll take at least two days to get there on foot."

"Oh, I've got an idea about that. One I've even used in the past."

Cochran's face screwed up in thought for a couple of seconds. "Ah ha! You're talking about that sand schooner thing you built to chase after your kidnapped princess when you first crashed on Aashla."

"I am indeed. Captain Cochran, I know you want to bury your dead, but I'm afraid every minute I'm delayed could cost more lives. May I borrow the healthy members of your crew to help build it?"

"Mister Yarrow!" Cochran's first mate materialized beside his Captain. "Gather a work crew and do as Mr. Rice instructs."

The *Wind Dancer's* crew worked quickly and efficiently, following my instructions without question. Building the sand schooner within sight of the cloth-draped bodies of three of their fellow crewmen and using supplies salvaged from the wreck of their airship was all the motivation the men needed. Every man working with me volunteered to come with me and watch my back and every man accepted my rejection with a nod of acknowledgement.

We finished the sand schooner late in the afternoon. Several of the less injured crewmen presented me with a sail made from envelope patching cloth and two more gave me a bundle of supplies, including some precious water.

With the whole crew watching, I seated myself on the schooner and ran up the sail. The wind, freshening as the light faded, filled the sail and the sand schooner rolled forward. Cochran offered a salute with the men following suit. I gave a two-fingered salute in return. Then the sail caught the wind and I accelerated away from the crew and wreckage of the *Wind Dancer*.

The sand schooner rolled along at a steady speed, slowly but surely eating up the miles between me and the rogue galactic base. Piloting the craft took minimal concentration, giving me plenty of time to consider what Raoul had told me. The dying man hadn't understood everything he'd heard, but I understood it all.

Our two rogue galactics, Thor and Freya—pseudonyms, for sure—claimed to be members of Action For Indigenous Peoples, a political gadfly group. AFIP members—'fippers,' to everyone else-—believe the Federation has a poor record of protecting primitive species who have the misfortune to have their worlds discovered and colonized by humans. I'm honest enough to admit they have a point, and that AFIP's political wing has helped push through some badly needed legislation to protect primitive sentients.

The trouble is, not all fippers are content to work through the political process. The organization has a radical fringe that believes humans simply can't live in peace with any other intelligent species, and their most fanatical people have become terrorists, smuggling illegal weapons onto primitive worlds and stirring up native rebellions and massacres in hopes of driving the human colonists out.

The political wing of AFIP officially disavows the terrorists, of course. But now I had a pretty good idea of where Thor and Freya had come from and why they were here.

Raoul didn't know their full plan, and I doubt if even he would have gone along with it if he had. But they'd promised him the throne of Tarteg in exchange for his help using the Tartegian Navy to transport their bands of armed trogs around the world, and while Raoul thought Thor and Freya were crazy and their plan would never work, he'd convinced himself it was worth it to pretend to throw in with them, in order to win the throne before everything went to hell.

I agreed with Raoul that Thor and Freya's plan was doomed to failure. I disagreed that he'd ever had a chance of winning the throne of Tarteg. But a lot of trogs and humans were going to die before Thor and Freya were stopped, if someone didn't stop the madness before it got started.

Someone had to fight for trogs and humans alike. Someone had to make Thor and Freya answer for the laws they'd broken and the people they'd murdered.

That someone was me, David Rice, Prince Consort to Her Royal Highness Princess Callan of Mordan. And, not coincidentally, Scout First Class of the Terran Federation Exploration Corps.

A RASH DECISION

Callan

Ducking back down below the piece of wreckage we'd anchored the pinnace to, I said, "Everyone stay down and out of sight! That strange airship is coming this way and we don't want any members of the crew spotting people moving around down here."

"We're in a desert, Your Highness and haven't sufficient provisions to reach civilization," Mrs. Sune complained. "Surely surrender is a reasonable alternative!"

"Mrs. Sune, do you truly believe these people will simply hold you in accustomed comfort until a proper ransom can be arranged?" I didn't even try to keep the incredulity out of my voice. "Have you even bothered to take a look at the wreckage all around you?"

"Airships crash all the time," the woman persisted. "For all you know, those people in that strange airship rescued the survivors!"

"Madam, *those people* intentionally wrecked three airships of the Mordanian Navy last night, including my own ship. Were it not for my husband's ability to Boost, I would have died in that crash. Our three-man crew *did* die." I hissed while stalking toward the merchant's wife. From the way the woman retreated before me,

I've no doubt I came with eyes blazing. "On top of that, *those people* sent trogs armed with blaster rifles to attack and capture the survivors of the airship that came closest to their base. I watched the trogs gun down disoriented and wounded men who never even knew they were under attack. Then they rounded up the healthiest survivors and took them prisoner."

Mrs. Sune's retreat stopped when I backed her against the pinnace. I kept coming until I stood nose-to-nose with her.

"P-perhaps they'll treat civilians decently? After all, *we* won't be trying to attack them!"

"If you wish to take your chances with *those people*, I can assure you neither the Cochrans nor I will stop you—but don't count on your civilian status to protect you." I drew a finger across my throat and added, "The two galactics in charge of *those people* slit the throats of ten of their fellow galactic."

The blood drained from Mrs. Sune's face and she rather dramatically fainted. Mr. Sune, caught unprepared, utterly failed to catch his wife as she collapsed.

I spun away from the pair, only to find Mrs. Cochran's abnormally pale face staring at me as she pulled Sasha close to her. "Did these people truly murder their own co-workers?"

I nodded, releasing a long sigh. "They will not get the opportunity to do the same to us, Mrs. Cochran. Once that airship returns to its base, we'll find your husband and David. Barring that, we'll find one of the other Mordanian wrecks and rally the survivors. By the time the Terran Federation arrives on the scene, I fully expect we'll have this situation well in hand."

We all fell silent as the airship drew closer. Six pairs of eyes—Mrs. Sune resolutely maintained her faint—stared out of the shade cast by the wreck, watching for Raoul's strange vessel. Seconds later, the airship flew into view and I released the breath I'd been holding. The ship was a good mile from our hiding place and driving hard on our old course. A couple of minutes later, it flew out of sight and we settled down to wait for darkness.

Hours later, with the sun descending, we heard the distant sound of the airship returning. We never even spotted it and soon the sound faded away entirely. As the light faded, we winched the envelope back to its normal flying position, released the anchors, and Jade took us up.

Our young pilot made a beeline for the last place we'd seen the *Wind Dancer*. Gasps rose from all four Cochrans when we caught sight of the wrecked merchant ship.

"Is Daddy all right?" Sasha asked her mother, her voice fearful.

"I'm sure he is, honey," Mrs. Cochran replied as she blinked away tears.

A small crowd gathered as the pinnace reached the wreck. The Cochrans relaxed just a bit when they caught sight of Captain Cochran hobbling around with a makeshift crutch. My own heart slowly rose into my throat as I looked in vain for any sign of David.

As soon as Jade cut the power to the propeller, I leaned over the railing and called, "Where is David? Is he all right?"

"Don't you worry, Your Highness!" Captain Cochran called. "Your husband is fine. He's gone out to scout the enemy's base, is all."

"Oh, yes, that news is *such* a relief, Captain Cochran. Thank you ever so much."

"You're more than welcome, Your Highness!" Cochran's hearty response contrasted sharply with my own dry tone.

Mrs. Cochran laid a hand on my shoulder. "Sarcasm is wasted on men at times like these, Callan."

Jade tied quick-release knots through a ring using two lengths of rope. She dropped the two ropes off each side of the pinnace and the crew slowly pulled the pinnace toward the ground. To the Sunes' consternation, the little airship's keel struck desert while the railing was still six feet off the ground. A dozen crewmen helped the couple climb down without falling. Mrs. Cochran handed Sasha down while Will simply jumped. Then Jade and I helped Mrs. Cochran down into the waiting hands of the crew.

Throughout this process, Captain Cochran filled me in on what happened leading up to and after the crash. I felt a pang of regret at the news of Raoul's death, though more for the sorrow it would cause Rupor than for the Spare Prince, himself.

"You're next, Your Highness," Captain Cochran said.

"I'm not getting off here," I said. "Jade can give me a quick lesson in piloting this thing and then I'm going after my husband. Perhaps I can catch him before he reaches that mountain. Then the two of us will go in search of other Mordanian survivors."

"David said you'd insist on doing just that," Cochran said, "but he wants you to stay here. I promised him I'd keep you safe until he returns."

"You shouldn't make promises you can't keep, Captain," I replied. I leaned over the railing and added, "You're a married man. Does your wife always do what you say?"

The crew laughed and their captain joined in with them. Jade stepped up next to me, grinning and clapping me on the back.

"Hey, Dad," she called over the laughter, "catch!"

Then Jade shoved me over the railing and into the waiting arms of the crew.

"Well done, daughter!" Cochran said. "Now—Jade! What do you think you're doing?"

Staring straight up from the arms of the crew, I had a great view as Jade pulled her two quick-release knots. As the ropes slipped free, the pinnace shot up another ten feet.

"It's simple, Dad. Callan is right that someone should go find David," Jade smile and wave at us. "But that someone should be an experienced pilot."

I couldn't fault the girl's logic, just her choice in pilots. "Jade, there's bound to be someone else who can pilot that pinnace just as well as you can! Don't do this to your parents!"

"I know what David looks like but you don't know what my boyfriend looks like. I'm the only one who will keep an eye out for Forbose." Jade engaged the propellers and the pinnace swung around toward the mountain off in the distance. "Don't worry! I promise I'll be careful!"

The girl's father, mother, and I all yelled, "Jade, no!"

Then the pinnace sped off in pursuit of my husband and Jade's boyfriend.

NOWHERE TO HIDE

David

J ust before night fell, the last rays of sunlight streaming over the mountains glinted off of something in the air far ahead of me. The object's speed left no doubt it was the anti-grav airship, now under the command of the self-proclaimed god of thunder. Considering the man had a weather control machine, I guess there was some merit to his claim. Still, his hubris rubbed me the wrong way. Since coming to Aashla, I've precipitated the downfall of princes, criminal underlords, and space pirates. It was time to add a pair of false gods to the list.

The desert floor was fully dark and the dust the sand schooner threw into the air merged into the mountains behind me. With luck, spotting it from such a distance would be all but impossible. As I watched the airship speed through the darkening sky, the implications of its course hit me like one of Thor's proverbial thunderbolts. The airship's flight path traced back to the course the *Wind Dancer's* pinnace took when Jade piloted it and its precious cargo away from the doomed merchant ship! Without Raoul—well known for his obsession with me—in command of the airship, Thor obviously set off after the pinnace. But could they catch it after all the time spent chasing the *Dancer*? Did Jade alter her course once her ship was out of sight of the chase?

I knew in my bones Callan would have advocated a course change in the hopes of learning how the pursuit of the *Wind Dancer* ended. Did they end up flying right into the path of the other airship? Were Callan, Jade, and the rest of the passengers now prisoners on the very airship my eyes tracked across the sky?

The logical part of my brain interrupted this worrisome emotional train of thought. It combined what I knew of the fipper fringe mindset with what I knew about Raoul. From allowing Raoul to pursue me to abandoning and killing Raoul when he found himself unable to capture me, Thor's actions struck me as surprisingly Raoul-like in nature. So, what would Raoul do if he captured Callan and Captain Cochran's family? Without a doubt, Raoul would return to the wrecked *Wind Dancer*, both to gloat and to force my surrender. Logically, that meant Thor did not hold Callan and the others captive.

Logic and emotion argued back and forth, with neither fully suppressing the other. In the end, I tried my best to push the question from my mind and concentrate on getting into Thor's base. And that problem kept my mind busy for the rest of my ride. That ride took me past the ruins of our original airship. Though the crash happened the previous night, it felt as long ago as the morning we'd set out on our tour of the research stations.

I steered the sand schooner toward a patch of scraggly bushes at the base of the mountain, lowering the sail as I rolled up to it. I resisted the urge to charge headlong up the mountain and spent half an hour partially dismantling the schooner and hiding it as best I could in the bushes. By the time I was finished, it wasn't likely the schooner would be spotted from the air, though a foot patrol would find it easily enough. Without a backward glance, I started up the mountain.

I was most definitely *not* returning to the cave I visited hours ago during the morning. It was watched and also was, according to Raoul, a trap just waiting for me to step into it. He told me of another entrance, one I could reach by circling around the mountain in the opposite direction from the cave. I knew nothing else beyond Raoul's brief directions as he rushed to tell me as much as possible before dying from Boost Burnout.

Unsure what awaited me, I spiraled up the mountain, angling well away from the cave mouth. I'll be honest, the climb nearly did me in. In normal circumstances, I'd have slept for hours after my Boosted run up the other side of this same mountain to catch up to the *Wind Dancer* as she passed over the mountaintop. Instead, I got almost fifteen entire minutes of rest before Callan was forced to wake me up. Since then, I'd remained on the go and even Boosted a second time for my duel with Raoul. My muscles ached and I desperately wanted to curl up under some bushes and sleep until sunrise. But I had to view this other entrance to their base before resting so I'd at least know what I was up against when I woke up.

So I stumbled and staggered up and around the mountain, past piles of boulders and more of the slippery screes that are all over this wasteland of a mountain. I found myself stopping for a rest every thirty minutes. Then it was every twenty minutes. Soon, I was resting five minutes out of every fifteen and struggling mightily to stay awake. But I finally found myself approaching the back side of the mountain and staggering toward its crest.

That's when I heard trog voices coming from around a bend in the trail. Realizing they were heading my way, I looked about for a place to hide. In an unsurprising end to a day in which very little had gone right for me, I was caught in the middle of a large patch of barren mountainside. With trogs only a few dozen yards away, I had no place to hide.

ON DAVID'S TRAIL

Callan

Mrs. Cochran watched the pinnace speed off into the gathering darkness. "Lon, what are we going to do? I can't lose my girl!"

Captain Cochran put an arm around his wife and gave her a squeeze. "Pray and hope, Nell."

Without bothering to lower her voice, Mrs. Sune said, "Well, I'm hardly surprised. Her parents let her run wild around the ship, doing men's work and wearing men's clothing. I mean, pants? I ask you!"

Mrs. Cochran stiffened and her husband whispered to her, "Ignore the woman, Nell. It won't help Jade. On top of that, we may not have a ship right now, but when our new one is built we'll sail under the Oshwindon flag."

"No, Captain Cochran," I said, "you'll sail under the Mordanian flag unless you choose otherwise." The Captain looked at me in surprise, I added, "All fees waived and without waiting in the lists."

Cochran kissed his wife's hand lovingly. "In that case, if it will make you feel better, Nell, please give the Sunes a taste of the temper you've held in check these last two weeks."

The Sunes were already backing away from the couple as a ghost of a smile crossed Mrs. Cochran's face. "I've already said enough. Besides, it won't help Jade." She looked at one of the crewmen arrayed rather menacingly behind the nervous couple. "Mister Yarrow, please take the Sunes somewhere where decent folk can neither see nor hear them. I don't want to catch sight of them again before my daughter is safely returned."

"Aye aye, ma'am." The second-in-command took the Sunes in hand, leading them away from us. Over his shoulder, he added, "Don't you worry about Miss Jade, ma'am. She's a smart and capable young lady."

"Thank you, Mister Yarrow," she replied.

"And don't forget that David is out there," I said. "If she does find him, rest assured he'll take care of her."

Mrs. Cochran's tentative smile returned, "Well, *that* would certainly please Jade no end! But my daughter can be quite head-strong and impulsive—she might be more than your husband can handle."

"She sounds remarkably like someone David knows extremely well." I smiled at the Cochran's puzzled expressions. "Jade sounds like me. David has managed to keep me alive through many trials and tribulations. He'll do the same for your daughter."

The Cochrans looked off into the darkness as if hoping for one last glimpse of the pinnace and its pilot. When they turned back to face me, it was as the captain and lady of the *Wind Dancer*. They issued orders and, within minutes, had a cooking fire and a larger signal fire burning.

Young Will eyed the fires with concern. "Should we have fires, Callan? In all the adventure stories Jade read to me and the ones I read for myself, the hero never builds a fire at night because it will give away his position to the bad guys."

I laid a hand on the lad's shoulder. "The bad guys already know where we are, Will. They're the ones who crashed your family's airship."

"Right... So Daddy—" The boy gave me a sidelong glance at the use of the word for his father. "So, um, *Dad* hopes some good guys spot the fire?"

"Exactly. And you know you don't have to be ashamed of calling your father 'Daddy.' I still use that name for my father."

"Yeah, but you're a *girl*," Will scoffed.

I suppressed a laugh. "Well, I can't argue with that logic! Don't worry, Will, your little slip of the tongue is safe with me."

Then Mrs. Cochran called the boy to help her prepare dinner. When I volunteered to help, the woman shook her head in horror at my suggestion. "Goodness, Your Highness, what kind of hosts do you take us for?"

"Practical ones, I hope," I said. "Look, Nell—may I call you Nell?"

"Of course, Your Highness!"

"Thank you. And you must remember to call me Callan." I looked at all the activity going on around me. "Nell, you've got more to do than you have hands to do it. There's no sense in having one pair of hands sitting idle just because they're at the end of a princess's arms." Nell hesitated for a second, so I added, "Don't make me use my princess glare on you!"

"Very well, Callan," Nell raised her hands in mock surrender. She gave me an appraising look, obviously trying to figure out what task she could safely assign to me. "Um, what would you like to do?"

"What you really mean is what *can* I do without ruining it."

"I'd never have put it so indelicately, Callan," Nell grinned, "but yes, that is what I meant."

"I've been known to stir pots without ruining their contents and can ladle food onto plates with the best of them," I replied.

The simple tasks kept me busy and the next hour passed quickly. By the time everyone was fed and everything cleaned up, the crew seemed willing to accept me as one of the family. After that, Captain Cochran led a brief memorial service for the three crewmen who died in the crash. I mentally added the names of the airmen from my little airship, those lost from the *Vanguard*, and most especially young Chris during the prayers.

Captain Cochran was five words into the final prayer for the dead when the wind carried a distant sound to our ears. An airship was approaching from the east!

Cochran fell silent for a few seconds, balancing on his makeshift crutches, listening to the sound of the airship's engines. He gave a nod and resumed his prayer for the dead. It ended with the entire crew voicing "Amen," after which everyone remained quiet, heads bowed, perhaps privately adding their own words to the Captain's or simply remembering friends now gone.

Respecting the solemnity of the moment, I added my own prayer for the *Wind Dancer's* three lost crewmen. When the crew stirred and the gathering broke apart, I waited while Cochran exchanged words with any member of the crew who wished to speak with him. After the last crewman wandered back to the fire, I approached the Captain.

"God knows I realize just how inadequate words are at this time, Captain Cochran, but I am deeply sorry for your losses." Unbidden, my mind brought forth images of all the men who gave their lives to save mine. I blinked rapidly to clear away the tears that always accompanied those memories.

"Thank you, Your Highness. And I've no doubt you know equally well that it's the thoughts behind the inadequate words that truly matter. Your thoughts are written plainly on your face." Captain Cochran smiled sadly, his gentle eyes meeting my own. "But much as you wish to offer comfort, I'm sure you have other matters on your mind."

"I'm afraid you're right, Captain. What did your nod mean after you stopped the prayer and listened to the airship?"

"I don't know whose airship approaches, Your Highness, but it's not the one that flies without an envelope."

"You can tell that just by the sound of the engines?" I didn't even try to keep the awe out of my voice.

"I've been sailing the skies of Aashla since I was a lad, Your Highness. I've picked up a trick or two during those years." Cochran turned to the east and looked off into the night sky. "The engines on the airship that wrecked the *Dancer* sounded quieter than they should have. That's because the noise didn't echo off the envelope, as it would on any other airship. Taking distance into account, the engines driving the airship coming this way sound normal to my ears. That means it has an envelope."

"Do you think they'll offer their help?"

"Likely they will. This route is too lightly traveled for raiders to waste time on it and no reputable captain would refuse help to a crew in need." Cochran looked at his family and then me, before adding, "That said, I'd prefer you and my family get under cover until we're sure of their intentions."

I nodded in agreement and allowed a crewman to guide Nell, Will, Sasha, and me into the shelter of a mostly-intact piece of the *Wind Dancer*. To my relief, Captain Cochran did not put us in the same place he'd stored the Sunes. We sat quietly, listening as the engine noise grew louder. We even looked up, as if trying to see through the timbers blocking our view of the sky.

Nell remained outwardly calm for the benefit of her children. Imagining how I'd react if my own Rob and Anne were with me, I strove to match her equanimity. So intent were we upon the sounds of the airship, we both jumped visibly when a crewman poked his head into our shelter and spoke.

"Cap'n says it's okay to come on out, ladies."

I followed the Cochrans out into the open. Looking up into a night sky lit by the bright band of the planetary ring arching over us, I laid eyes on a most welcome sight.

A mighty airship floated no more than fifty feet above us. Green flags bearing a golden falcon snapped and fluttered in the wind, stirring my heart even more than the Mordanian flag normally does. Several officers clustered at the bow, one of them pointing my way.

Captain Jorson, Naval Commander of my expedition, and his miraculously-undamaged airship, the *Tercel*, had found us. More importantly, the intact warship indicated an intact crew—including a full contingent of Marines.

Captain Jorson slid down a quickly lowered rope and bowed

before me. "I cannot put into words my relief at finding you alive and well, Your Highness! When we saw that freak storm knock the *Vanguard* from the sky, we feared the worst for you."

Remembering the airship crash and David's frantic, Boost-enhanced efforts to keep the two of us alive, I shuddered. "By a miracle and David's quick reactions, he and I survived the crash. Our crewmen did not. Many of the *Vanguard's* crew died in their crash—as well, and many more were killed when trogs attacked them."

Jorson rose quickly from his bow and fixed his intense stare on me. "Is the Great One on the march again? I thought he liked Captain Rice and Your Highness."

"No, I'm positive this has nothing to do with the Great One, Captain. I'm rather unclear about who is behind all of this, but it's not him." As quickly as possible, I outlined the events of the previous twenty-four hours. I told what little I knew of David's actions after we split up and then got Captain Cochran to add what little he knew.

Wrapping up the tale, I asked, "And what of the *Tercel*, Captain? How did you keep the wind from dashing your airship to the ground like it did to the *Vanguard* and my ship?"

"Credit for that goes to my second-in-command, Your Highness. He was the officer of the watch when we spotted the *Vanguard* in distress. He immediately ordered the ship to land, deflate the envelope, and anchor the airship." Jorson gave a self-deprecating smile. "I relieved the man from duty when I learned what he ordered. The storm struck before the guards even got Lieutenant Tucker below deck. I rode out that horrible windstorm wondering just how many members of my crew Tucker saved with his quick thinking."

I nodded, looking at the huge envelope strung above the *Tercel's* hull. "And you spent most of the time since then re-inflating the envelope?"

"Just so, Your Highness. Of course, we only had heated air

available to refill *Tercel's* envelope rather than proper gas, so she flies low in the sky. But she flies!"

"The important thing is that you're here, Captain. How many men do you have in total?"

"Three hundred and forty-six, including eighty Marines." A humorless smile played across the Captain's face. "I can assure you each and every one of them wants a go at those who downed their sister ships!"

"Excellent! Lift me onboard and we can set off after David."

My request took Captain Jorson by surprise. "I do not believe that is wise, Your Highness. You should stay here, where you will be safe. Once we've found Captain Rice or subdued the trogs, we'll return for you."

I expected this argument and had my defense ready. "Do you know where you're going, Captain?"

Jorson pointed south along the edge of the mountain range. "It doesn't seem like a particularly complicated route, Your Highness."

"Perhaps I should rephrase the question. Do you know where you're *stopping*, Captain?"

That gave Jorson pause for a few seconds before he shrugged. "No, Your Highness, I do not know where we're stopping. I don't suppose you'd care to describe the mountain to me?"

"I'm not sure I can give you a description adequate to to your needs, Captain, but I'm absolutely positive I will recognize it when I see it."

"Somehow, I just *knew* you were going to say that, Your Highness. Will you at least promise to remain on board the airship when the fighting starts?" At my nod, Jorson turned back to his airship and called, "Lower a sling for Her Highness!"

I gave quick hugs to the Cochrans and promised to find Jade and keep her safe, as well. Then I was hoisted onto the *Tercel* and we sailed off to find my husband.

JADE TO THE RESCUE

David

With no place to hide and no energy to run, I did the only thing possible. I drew my sword, offered up a prayer for a miracle, and waited for the trogs to round the bend in the path.

Seconds later, four trogs walked into sight. Talking among themselves, they walked several feet before noticing me blocking their way. The four carried spears instead of the expected blaster rifles. Was this an answer to my prayer or had Thor made a point of examining all of the blaster rifles when he returned to base. Had he discovered just how filthy the guns were? Either way, the trogs regarded me quizzically for several long seconds before their leader handed his spear to one of the others. Holding his hands up to show he was unarmed, the trog took a couple of careful steps my way.

I readied my sword, which made the unarmed trog raise his hands higher and wave them back and forth in the human sign of negation. I relaxed my stance and lowered my sword, relieved the trog hadn't seen my arm shaking slightly from the exertion. A strange buzzing assailed my ears, no doubt further proof of my exhaustion.

The trog pointed at me with his left hand and then pointed to his right hand. Finally, he made a fist with his right hand and hit himself on the chest. He did this another time before turning a questioning look my way.

What the hell was this trog trying to say? My exhaustion fogged brain couldn't figure it out. I shook my head and shrugged. "I don't know what you mean."

The trog muttered something in his own language. I imagine it was along the lines of, "Why is this human so stupid?" Then he went through the entire pantomime a second time. When he hit himself on the chest, though, he added a theatrical head roll and his tongue lolled from his mouth.

As tired as I was, even I could figure out the trog was playing dead. With that minor realization, I caught onto another part of it. Careful not to appear threatening, I reversed my hold on my sword, ran it between my left arm and my body, and copied the tongue lolling.

The trog nodded and took a step my way. I jumped back and raised my sword again. "Whoa there! I didn't say you could just walk up and kill me."

The trog shook his head, gave me a dark look, and returned to his squad. Once again armed, he and his patrol readied their spears.

Damn my exhaustion! I'd obviously missed any chance to get out of this without fighting—that meant I'd probably missed any chance of getting out of this alive.

"He's asking if you're the Hand of Death."

The voice, young and feminine, came from above me. As one, the trogs and I looked up. Fifty feet over us floated the *Wind Dancer's* pinnace. Captain Cochran's daughter Jade stared down at us from the railing. How in God's name had we not heard the pinnace approaching? A trick of the rocks and wind? Simple exhaustion? I pushed aside those thoughts and focused my mind on the trogs.

The trog leader pointed at Jade, looked at me, and then nodded.

"Can you understand what I'm saying?" I asked. Trog vocal cords are very different from human ones, making it all but impossible for either race to speak the other's languages. But you don't have to speak a language to understand it.

The trog nodded.

"And you were asking if I am the human the Great One calls the Hand of Death?" When the trog nodded, I said, "Yes, I am that human."

The trog immediately launched into a far more elaborate pantomime. Within seconds, I was completely baffled.

"Hey, trog," Jade called from the little airship, "do you know the trade signs?"

With a look of considerable relief, the trog nodded.

Jade vented gas from the pinnace's envelope, bringing the little craft closer to the ground. "Let me land this thing and then I'll translate for you."

I scanned the pinnace's railing for signs of Callan. Seeing none, I asked, "Where is my wife?"

"When we reached the wreck of the *Dancer*, Captain Dad insisted she stay with him and the crew." The girl's voice broke slightly when she mentioned the airship whose name she selected. "He didn't really want to let me come after you, but we had to know if you were safe."

"Remind me to thank your father for both keeping Callan safe and sending you to check on me. How did he convince my wife to stay behind?"

"He didn't. As I lowered the pinnace, Her Highness was leaning over the rail arguing with my father over his plan. Mom and the others had already slid down lines to the ground, so I gave a signal to Dad and pushed the princess overboard. You can tell she grew up around airships because she can swear like an airman when she's angry."

Jade hopped lightly from the pinnace when it touched down. She and the trog exchanged gestures for a minute or so before Jade turned to me. "The short version is the trogs are honored to meet the Hand of Death and don't want to test the truth of your name. In fact, they really just want to get away from the crazy humans—those are my words, the trog called them 'sun touched'—and go home."

I turned to the trog leader. "If I let you go in peace, will you tell the Great One about this place? We may need his help before this is over."

All four of the trogs nodded emphatically and hurried past me. Jade and I watched them trot along the path and disappear from sight.

"It's a good thing trogs can't read human body language," Jade said. "Could you have beaten them in your current condition?"

"Probably not. So allow me to thank you doubly for your timely intervention." I kissed the girl's hand and was rewarded with a blush and a giggle. "And now, m'lady, you should return to your father and report my condition to him."

"You can't send me away now! What if you need another translation? I-"

The buzzing I'd heard earlier returned, stronger and much louder than before. It drowned out Jade's protests and we both looked around for the source. A hundred yards away, a glowing silver ball emerged from the top of a rock chimney. Tiny lightning bolts flashed from the ball and off into the sky. Within seconds, a stiff wind sprang up, rocking the grounded pinnace.

Jade broke for the airship as soon as it moved. I caught her arm and pulled her back.

"Let go! I've got to get my pinnace away from this storm!"

I pointed to the silver ball. "It's not a natural storm, Jade. The wind is just getting started. When it reaches full power, it will smack that pinnace out of the sky as easily as you could swat a bug. We've got to find cover *now* or it might even blow us off of this mountain."

Jade gave the pinnace a forlorn look then followed me along the path. We were still out in the open when the full brunt of the wind struck.

ANOTHER STORM

Callan

I stood in the bow of the *Tercel* accompanied by Captain Jorson and an ensign with a spyglass. Captain Jorson kept the airship no more than seventy feet off the ground, choosing to forego the advantages of altitude for the advantages of a quick landing. During the first part of the journey, I gave the Captain my third-hand explanation of what was going on. Jorson listened attentively to everything Captain Cochran told me about everything Raoul told David. The Captain's face grew graver with each passing moment.

"If I understand this, Your Highness, these galactics have figured out how to install one of those implant machines and give a man Boost, just like Captain Rice has?"

"It appears so," I replied. "I know that is supposed to be classified information in the Terran Federation, but you know as well as I do that secrets of that nature eventually get out."

Jorson nodded, conceding the point. "They've also figured out how to smuggle their blaster weapons onto Aashla in pieces and have armed men and trogs with the weapons. And if all of that weren't enough, they've got some kind of machine that creates windstorms so violent they knock large warships out of the sky. Is that about it?"

"Begging the Captain's pardon, sir, you left out the airship that flies without an envelope," the Ensign added.

"Yes, thank you, Ensign Bodver," Jorson growled. "Since you've obviously been listening to our discussion, perhaps you would be so good as to tell me what you should be on the lookout for?"

"The strange airship, obviously, sir." Bodver appeared unfazed by his Captain's demand and answered without taking his eye from his spyglass. "But I think the strange glowing ball that shoots off little lightning bolts is the main concern. Does Her Highness know where on the mountain this ball will be found?"

"I only got a quick look at it," I said, "but it was near the top of the mountain, Ensign Bodver."

"Very good, Ensign," Jorson said. "Sing out if you see the wreck of the *Vanguard* or that glowing ball."

"Aye aye, sir!"

"Captain, might I offer a suggestion?" I asked quietly.

"You are my princess, Your Highness. You command, should you so desire."

"I would only consider commanding in the direst of emergencies, Captain Jorson. The *Tercel* is your ship and you know her and her crew far better than I." Jorson smiled, inclining his head slightly at my comment. I continued, "If Ensign Bodver spots that glowing ball, it's imperative the *Tercel* land as quickly as possible. May I suggest you pass word that the crew treat the Ensign's warning as an order to land?"

Jorson gave a sharp nod. "I should have thought of that, Highness. I'll pass the word."

Fortunately, the night sky provided more light than it had years ago when I sailed into Beloren under the cover of darkness to rescue David. Unfortunately, my night sight was no better than it was all those years ago. The Ensign had much better eyes.

"Captain Jorson, I see the glowing ball!"

The crew, already poised for landing procedure, leapt into action. Men pulled out anchor lines and heavy mallets. Others vented gas from the envelope and the big ship settled toward the ground. The engine crew dowsed the fire in the boilers, leaving the airship running on the remaining pent-up steam.

Even with the crew's rapid response, the wind whipped up quickly. The taut rigging thrummed as the storm blew around them and the airship bucked in the driving wind. We were ten feet from the ground when the wind caught the envelope and pulled the ship back up into the air.

"It's going to be dangerous landing in these conditions, sir!" an officer shouted over the wind. "If we're not careful, the wind will catch the envelope and wreck us. It might also pull us higher before doing so!"

Jorson gave his officer a sharp nod. "Have crew stand by to cut the envelope loose—but not until I give the order!"

The officers relayed the command around the airship. Dozens of knife-wielding crewmen ran to stays, ready to saw away at the lines should the order come. Meanwhile, the helmsman worked the ailerons, trying to drive the airship as close to the ground as possible.

"Ensign Bodver," Jorson yelled over the wind, "Do you see any possible cover from this wind?"

The young man lowered his spyglass and looked about the ship. A few seconds later, his arm shot out, pointing to starboard. "There, sir! A small alcove in the foot of the mountain!"

Captain Jorson didn't even look where Bodver was pointing. "Helmsman—hard to starboard and follow the Ensign's directions!"

Jorson took my arm and pulled me into the meager protection of an inner railing. "Stay here, away from the outer railing, Highness. It's safer." He turned to a nearby crew member. "Airman, protect the princess until we're safely down!"

"Aye, sir!" Covering my body with his own, the airman shouted, "Pardon my familiarity, Your Highness."

"There's no pardon necessary," I replied as I wrapped my arms around the airman and buried my head against his chest.

All around me the lines sang with the wind, snapping and

popping as the envelope bucked in the wind. And then comparative silence descended as the *Tercel* sailed into the small alcove and out of the worst of the wind.

Officers shouted orders and the mighty airship dropped to the ground with a bone-jarring thump.

"Winch the envelope down, men! Quickly!"

A minute later, the envelope was nestled down on top of the *Tercel*, seriously cutting into our headroom. But the ship was down, safe, and intact.

But what of David and Jade? Was the pinnace caught by the storm? Watching the wind roar around us, I could only wonder and worry.

SCOUTING MISSION

David

The wind pushed against Jade and me like a giant hand, driving us backward. Sand and grit scoured every inch of exposed skin, opening dozens of scrapes. Small rocks hit all over our bodies, their jagged edges opening larger cuts that soon filled with dust and dirt.

Jade's arms suddenly flailed as the wall of air pushed her off balance. I caught her around the waist and pulled her to my side. I spun the two of us around so the worst of the wind struck our backs then put my mouth to Jade's ear.

"Stay low, keep your back to the wind, and don't let go of me." I couldn't even hear my own shout over the wind, but Jade nodded her head. "Can you see any kind of shelter where we can hole up?"

In the dark and with all of the junk swirling in the air around us, I had little hope of finding any kind of cover—and I was partially right. I found myself putting what little energy I had left into keeping the wind from blowing Jade and me off the top of the mountain. But Jade, better rested and with younger eyes than mine, spotted something. Her arm shot out pointing to our right. I couldn't see anything that way, but I lowered my shoulders and shoved my way through the strengthening wind in the direction Jade pointed.

After fighting my way across the longest ten feet of ground I'd ever crossed, we came upon a boulder leaning against a sheer part of the mountainside. Jade pointed down and I saw there was a space between the boulder and the little cliff face. Kneeling, I all but pushed Jade into the crevice then rolled in after her. The wind and the dust still assailed my back, but my body shielded Jade from the worst of the storm and we could breathe freely.

The girl's face was right in front of mine, but I could barely see it. I felt her body trembling though I couldn't tell whether that was from the exertion, fear, or cold.

"Are you all right, Jade?"

She started at the sound of my voice and must have turned to face me. I felt short, shallow breath on my cheek. I pulled the girl close to me, offering the comfort of human contact. Her body was stiff as a board.

"Slow your breathing down, Jade. You'll feel better if you take long, deep breaths."

Gradually, the girl's breathing slowed and her body relaxed. Outside, the wind still howled, grit still got inside my shirt, and stones still smacked into my back. Inside, we had a small pocket of calm that slowly soothed Jade's nerves. After a few minutes, she turned her head and pressed it against my chest.

"I thought this would be more," Jade paused for a couple of seconds. "I guess romantic is the right word."

"Real adventures aren't romantic, Jade. Mostly, they're uncomfortable and terrifying."

"Um, yeah. That's what I meant."

Callan says I'm pretty dense when it comes to figuring out members of the opposite sex. I say that just means I'm no different than any other man. But for once, I actually put two and two together and figured out what Jade was talking about.

"You're not talking about adventures, are you? At least, not *just* adventures."

"I, uh, don't know what you're talking about."

"That's probably because I'm entirely wrong about something," I said.

Jade was quiet for about a minute before she said, "You're not wrong. I was talking about being rescued by you."

"We can pretend I was wrong anyway," I replied, "if you'd prefer that."

Jade gave a long sigh. "No. Besides, being rescued by someone like you is just a silly little girl's dream. It's time I grew up."

"First, *you* rescued me by saving me from fighting those trogs. I just helped you get out of the wind. Second, your dreams may change form as you get older, but that doesn't mean you have to abandon them."

"Huh?"

"There's a part of my story that isn't in any of the books or vids or songs people keep creating about me." I smiled though Jade couldn't see it. "I guess you could call the story *David Rice and the Search for the Spacebabe*."

Jade listened attentively and snickered in all the right places as I told her of my lifelong dream of finding adventure among the stars and how the dream evolved into finding my soulmate. When I wrapped up the story, she sighed and said, "That is so romantic and sweet and pretty much impossible for us normal people."

"Nothing in life is impossible, Jade. Believe in your dreams and they'll come true in ways you could never imagine or predict." I broke off for a huge yawn. "And now I really need to get some sleep."

With the wind still lashing my back, I dropped into a deep and desperately needed sleep.

I awoke with a start as I felt a hand covering my mouth. My eyes refused to spring open as gummy eyelids resisted my first attempts to pry them apart. Just as I wondered if Boost was required to force the lids apart, both of them slowly pulled apart.

"Shhhh!" Jade hissed.

As my brain came up to speed, I realized the girl's hand covered my mouth. I nodded slightly so she'd know I understood. I blinked to clear my eyes and my eyelids stuck briefly. The sticking eased with each blink, though my clearing vision revealed very little. Weak light from Aashla's ring filtered into our crevice, barely illuminating Jade's green eyes and blond hair a couple of inches in front of me.

The girl pulled her hand from my mouth and whispered in a tight voice, "I heard voices just now."

Keeping my voice as low as hers, I asked, "You're facing out—can you see anything?"

She lifted her head and, with worried eyes, peered past me. "Not really. I think the windstorm piled a lot of dirt and small rocks against your back."

Only when she mentioned the windstorm did I notice the wind no longer shrieked behind me. Then I heard the sound of feet walking through loose stone.

"What's with this foot search, Van? Ain't this what that fancy airship is fer?" The voice held the whiny tone of a born follower.

"The bat reez what run it be pleated so's they sent us." The second voice was both confident and exasperated. It reminded me of every know-it-all I'd ever met.

"Oh. Can it be repleated, Van?"

"Course it can, Frank. Didn't you listen up when we joined?"

The footsteps stopped not ten feet from us. I imagined Van looking at Frank in irritation.

"I tried, Van, but it didn't make no sense."

"They's got to…" Van paused as if trying to recall exact wording. "Uh, deploy the solar collectors. But they don't work if'n the sun ain't up."

"A'right, Van, but that don't splain what we's doing lookin' around up here. It ain't like we can pull the sun up."

"Damn, Frank, we ain't looking fer the sun. We's lookin' fer survivors from that little airship what the boss said was flyin' round this here mountain. Someone musta made it since them trogs what was guardin' up here done disappeared. Now come on."

The footsteps started again, heading down the mountain and away from us.

"I don't rightly mind much if'n them survivors kilt a few trogs, Van. Never liked workin' with them no how."

The voices faded as the men walked away so we barely heard Van's response.

"Shut up, Frank."

As the footsteps drew farther away, I whispered, "Well, there go a couple of born minions."

Jade snorted quietly and slapped a hand over her mouth. After composing herself, she whispered, "Don't *do* that! What if I'd laughed out loud and brought those two back here?"

Doing my best to imitate Frank's accent, I said, "Welp, I figger I could make 'em think they done found a talkin' rock. Or if'n they's got blaster rifles, I 'spect they'd probably shoot each other."

The girl clapped a hand over my mouth again. "Shut *up* before I really do start laughing!"

The exchange eased much of the girl's tension, so I did as she asked and changed the subject. "I want to get out of this crevice, but we'll only go if you're up to it. Did you get any sleep?"

"Yeah, I got enough sleep. It's not like I did anything really tiring today. Or yesterday."

"Good. You've got better ears than me. Can you hear anything out there?"

Jade listened intently for half a minute. "I can't hear anything. We're as clear as we're ever going to be, David."

I slowly swept an arm behind me, pushing debris away from my back. Then I rolled out over the remaining hump of stones and rose stiffly to my feet. I cleared more space for Jade and she wiggled out of the crevice. We both took a minute to stretch the kinks out of our muscles.

"Are you feeling okay, Jade?" At her nod, I continued, "Good. You need to work your way down the mountain and get back to your father. You've just got those two idiots to-"

Jade folded her arms and glared at me. "Oh no you don't, David

Rice! You need someone to watch your back up here. And if you run into any more trogs, who's going to tell them you're the Hand of Death?"

"I appreciate the offer, Jade, but there's no way I can take a teenage girl any closer to this place!"

"You've taken teenage boys on adventures before! Or did the stories get that wrong, too?" The girl's glare intensified when I shook my head. "Besides, I'm just going to double back and follow you as soon as you're out of sight. So either we both go back to my father or we both go on."

I blew out my breath in exasperation. "You sound just like Callan."

Jade grinned. "Thank you!"

"Fine, you can come—but only if you do *exactly* as I say. This is just a scouting mission. We're going close enough to get a look at what's going on and then we're leaving. Is that clear?"

"Yes sir!"

I walked in the direction the trogs and the two minions came from. "Stay close and stay quiet."

We slipped silently along the path, ears and eyes searching the area for any indication of guards. I was closer to my destination than I'd imagined. A couple of hundred yards later, we came to the top of a precipice. Looking over the edge, I saw a ladder attached to the rock. It descended to a ledge about thirty feet below us. The top of a second ladder was visible descending from the ledge. Most of that ladder lay in darkness, but I assumed more ladders allowed men and trogs to ascend from the desert floor a good two hundred feet below us.

Bright light spilled from the mouth of a large cave far below, illuminating the desert floor where sat the docking space for the anti-grav airship. Men in chains moved around the airship, cleaning it and making repairs. Even in the dim light, I recognized Mordanian naval uniforms on the men.

Just then Jade caught my arm. "Someone's coming up the path!"

Two voices conversing in low tones came from around the long curve in the trail. We had mere seconds to get out of sight before the owners of those voices came into view. Only, there was no place to hide at the end of the trail—no handy jumble of boulders, no crevices to slip into, nothing.

If the men had blaster rifles, they'd have us dead to rights. If they only had swords, I could almost certainly win past them though not before they raised the alarm. That meant I had to find a way to take them out quickly and quietly. That left us with only one place to go—down.

"Climb down the ladder, Jade. Do you think you can fit between the ladder and the cliff?"

The girl's eyes widened in surprise, but she took a quick look over the edge of the precipice and nodded.

"Good. Go down about ten feet then do that. Loop your arms through the rungs and hold tight once you're in place."

Having grown up on and around airships, Jade ignored the two hundred foot drop to the desert floor and climbed nimbly down the ladder. Once there was room, I followed her. Jade easily maneuvered to the back side of the ladder and threaded her arms and legs around the rungs. I breathed a sigh of relief knowing she wouldn't get knocked off the ladder if I were forced to throw anyone over the cliff.

The voices drew closer, talking in low tones and joking like men on a boring duty have done for thousands of years. "It's a good thing the boss sent us up the side of the mountain. Those two idiots going the other way couldn't find their own asses with both hands and a mirror."

"Yeah, but as my old sergeant use to say, there's a place for morons in every army." The man paused briefly for dramatic effect. "And that place is between you and the enemy crossbows."

The other man laughed. "I'll have to remember that one." The laughter stopped and the man raised his voice. "We saw the pile of dirt and stones you must have used to conceal yourself under that rock. Whoever you are, we know you came this way because we'd have seen you if you went down."

The man paused for a few seconds, probably giving me a chance to surrender peacefully. I looked down at Jade and held my finger to my lips. She nodded.

"There's no place for you to hide up here, so we know where you are. Why not save everyone lots of trouble and come on up? We're under orders to take prisoners if possible. Otherwise, we shoot to kill."

Another few seconds passed before I heard the pair resume walking toward the end of the trail. They stopped a few feet from the edge and I heard one of them get down on his hands and knees.

"Cover me."

The man crept to the edge. I made my move when the top of his head came into view.

Boost!

My implant poured adrenaline into my veins and time slowed. Above me, the man's eyes widened at the sight of me. Before he could even open his mouth, I punched him fast and hard in the throat. My blow crushed his windpipe, leaving the man's mouth opening and closing to no effect. He was already dead, his brain just hadn't gotten the message yet.

By instinct, the man's hands went to his throat. His chest dropped to the ground and the man's body started sliding over the edge. His partner gave a cry, grabbed the dying man's feet, and pulled him back from the cliff's edge. With the other guard distracted, I made my next move.

Grabbing the top rung of the ladder, I shoved off hard with my feet and swung feet first onto the edge of the cliff. The uninjured guard had just enough time to realize something was wrong before I kicked him hard under the chin. His head snapped back with an audible crack and the man collapsed, his body spasming in the throes of death.

I pulled the suffocating guard away from the edge and snapped his neck, giving him a few seconds respite from a particularly horrible way to die. Then I dropped Boost.

Both guards had carried blaster rifles, which I took. From the look of the guns, my lesson on weapon cleanliness impressed Thor. The rifles' delicate electronics were wrapped in airship envelope cloth—not as effective as the molded shells a Federation blaster had, but much better than leaving the rifles open to the elements.

"Jade?" I called in a low voice. "It's safe to come back up."

The girl didn't answer. My heart leapt into my throat for fear she'd lost her grip on the ladder. I rushed to the edge, praying I wouldn't spot her crumpled on the ledge at the end of the first ladder. I spotted her on the ledge, all right, but she wasn't injured in the least.

I got there just in time to see her swing onto the second ladder and climb down.

UNPLANNED ESCAPE

David

Swearing silently, I scrambled onto the ladder and climbed after Jade as quickly as possible. The rough-hewn wood of the ladder ruled out the old navy trick of gripping the sides of the ladder and sliding down. Somehow, I doubted a dozen splinters in each hand would prove helpful if more fighting was called for. I settled for taking two rungs at a time, hoping to catch up with the girl before anyone spotted her.

Changing ladders at the ledge, I saw that Jade remained well ahead of me. Growing up on airships, the height didn't bother her and the climbing barely slowed her down. Frustrated, I picked up my own pace, taking three rungs with each step.

"Jade!" I hissed as loudly as I dared. "Stop and tell me what's going on!"

She looked my way and I waved her back to me. She shook her head and pointed down. Another narrow ledge was below her, this one no more than fifty feet from the bottom of the cliff. Having set her terms, Jade turned away and resumed her descent. Cursing silently, I followed after her. Knowing Jade was stopping at the next ledge, I took two-rung steps the rest of the way down to her.

When I reached the ledge, Jade was stretched out on her stomach and gazing intently at the scene below. In other words, I wasted a perfectly good glare on the back of her head. I dropped onto my own stomach so we'd both be harder to spot, putting my face a foot from hers. Even then, the girl kept staring below. I gave the area a quick scan, saw nothing out of the ordinary, and brought my glare back to Jade.

Taking her chin in my hand, I turned her head so she faced me and hissed, "What do you think you're doing? Is this your idea of doing exactly as I say?"

The girl's eyes dropped from mine. "I know you told me to stay with you, but—"

"There are no 'buts' in this, Jade. This is a terribly dangerous situation made far more dangerous by you haring off like this!" Rather than continue berating her, I went right to my strongest argument. "Would you do something this reckless on the *Wind Dancer?*"

Jade's eyes blazed for a moment. "Of course not—someone could get hurt or killed! It would be... irresponsible." Jade hung her head. "I'm sorry."

"What made you do something so..." I was going to say 'stupid' but thought better of it. Jade was most definitely not stupid. "So impulsive?"

Jade turned her eyes back to the scene below. "I thought I saw someone I recognized."

I caught myself before telling her I saw dozens of people I knew and once again tempered my words. "Who did you see?"

"Forbose. He worked on another merchant airship and it went missing about a month ago. We took the course past this place so we could look for him and his ship." Jade laid her head down on her arms. "He's sort of my boyfriend."

"Ah, so I have competition for your affections."

Jade snorted a short laugh. "You're just a handsome fantasy for me and my friends. Sort of like Callan and all the boys I know—except the boys have it a lot worse for Callan."

"That makes sense. After all, she is the most beautiful woman on eight planets."

"Yeah, don't remind me. How can we girls hope to compete with Callan, even if she is nothing more than a fantasy for the boys?"

"Just be your smart, snarky, funny self. Any boy who doesn't appreciate that isn't worthy of you anyway." I turned my gaze down to the anti-grav airship and all the activity around it. "And mentioning boys appreciating you, do you see Forbose down there now?"

Jade stared hard at the cave mouth and desert floor, her eyes sweeping methodically back and forth over the scene. After a minute, her head rose up and her stare intensified. She pointed toward the right side of the mouth of the cave. I sighted along her arm and spotted a young man about Jade's age.

The boy lifted a small ladle out of a metal tub sitting at his feet, bringing the ladle to his mouth. After drinking his fill, he poured water over his head and let it run down his neck.

"That *is* Forbose!" Excitement drove Jade's voice from a whisper to a low speaking tone. "Oh, David, we've got to find a way to rescue him!"

Dropping the ladle back into the tub, Forbose bent over and picked up something leaning against the tub. As he rose, the light from the cave illuminated the object in the boy's hands. Forbose cradled one of Thor's blaster rifles.

Jade gasped. This time when she spoke, her voice was barely audible. "No. No. That can't be! Not Forbose!"

As the two of us watched, three men chained together staggered toward the tub. Forbose rose to his full height, brandished his blaster rifle, and stepped between the men and the tub. The three men argued or pleaded with Forbose, pointing several times at the tub of water. Jade's sort-of-boyfriend—almost certainly now her ex-sort-of-boyfriend—stood fast, waving for the men to go back to work on the airship. When the three didn't immediately leave, Forbose rammed the butt of his blaster rifle into the stomach of one of the men. The man doubled over and stumbled back into one of the other two men. They both tripped over the chains and fell down, leaving the third man in clear sight for the first time.

It was my turn to gasp as the light fell across the face of Ensign Chris Marlow!

"Chris is alive!" I hadn't even meant to say that aloud, but I couldn't help myself.

Jade looked away from the scene of her sort-of-boyfriend's bullying. "Who's Chris?"

"The only one of those three men your sort-of-boyfriend didn't knock down."

"My ex-sort-of-boyfriend, you mean." Disgust mingled with pain in Jade's voice. "Why did you think this Chris guy was dead?"

"He charged two dozen trogs to distract them long enough for Callan and me to get away." The scene replayed in my mind, including the two blaster shots I'd thought killed the courageous lad. Even with Chris standing not fifty yards from me, the memory still sent chills down my spine.

"Wow," Jade said, wonder replacing the pain her voice held just seconds ago. "That was really brave."

Below, Chris helped the two Mordanian airmen to their feet, studiously ignoring the insults Forbose hurled at his back. The two older men staggered to their feet, exhaustion and thirst weighing heavily on them. Chris's face burned with anger, but he just pointed his two chain-gang companions toward the anti-grav airship.

All work on the airship came to a standstill as Forbose verbally lashed Chris. In the night air, without the sounds of work to mask it, Forbose's next barb carried clearly to us.

"Yeah, slink away boy. That's what I'd expect from the bastard get of some dockside doxy!"

All expression drained from Chris's face, along with most of the blood. His back slowly straightened, his shoulders flexed, and his hands balled into tight fists.

I unslung one of the two blaster rifles from my back and shoved it into Jade's hands. "Have you ever shot a crossbow?"

Taking the blaster, the startled girl nodded.

"Good. Aim the rifle like a crossbow except you can ignore wind and gravity. Then just pull the trigger."

Below, Chris spun around, putting all of his strength and momentum behind his punch. Blood burst from Forbose's nose as Chris's fist smashed it flat. The bigger boy staggered back, shocked at this sudden attack. Forbose's blaster rifle flew from his hands, landing well away from the four men.

"You're rescuing Chris?" Jade asked. At my nod, she added, "Good. Who do I shoot?"

"Anyone who looks like they need shooting, especially if I point at them with my sword," I said, swinging onto the ladder down to the desert floor.

Chris shuffled forward to hit his tormentor again. With anger clouding his judgement, the Ensign forgot the chains tethering him to the other two airmen. The links stopped his feet and Chris fell to the ground. He caught himself with his hands, but he now lay at Forbose's feet.

"Got it," Jade said as if my instructions made all the sense in the world. "If I knew your plan, it would be easier to pick helpful targets."

"And if I had a plan, I'd tell it to you."

Shouts erupted from below as the fight attracted more attention. I longed to turn and see what was happening to Chris, but I had to concentrate on the ladder if I had any hope of reaching the bottom in time to help. Even hopping down three rungs at a time, it felt as if minutes passed before I reached the ground even though my implant told me it was no more than half a minute.

I feared the eruption of blaster fire from the cave with every passing second. When my feet touched ground without hearing it, I wondered if Thor might still be cleaning and wrapping most of the blaster rifles. It wasn't the only explanation—perhaps the man simply didn't care if the guards and prisoners mixed it up a bit—but I fervently hoped my explanation was right.

By the time my feet hit the ground, the shouting drowned out most other sounds. Sprinting to the airship, I climbed over the railing and onto the deck. I also got my first look at the fight between Forbose and Chris since I left Jade. Blood covered Chris's face, streaming from a gash above one eye and a cut lip. Pain forced the Ensign into a crouch, probably from bruised or broken ribs. Blood still dripped from Forbose's nose and he had the makings of an excellent black eye. Despite having his mobility seriously compromised by the chains, Chris was putting up quite a fight.

I grabbed the first airman I came to, yelling so he could hear me over the shouts, "Where's an officer?"

The airman glanced at me and his eyes fairly popped out of his head. "Captain Rice, you're safe! Is Her Highness-?"

"Safe and unharmed. But where's an officer?"

"Of course, sir." The man turned and led me to the railing. "Captain Wright? Sir, it's Captain Rice!" Raising his voice even more, the airman called, "And Her Highness is safe and well!"

A ragged cheer rose from the men. Captain Wright spun around so fast I half expected the man to get dizzy. He wasted no time with small talk. "What's the plan, sir?"

I shoved the blaster rifle into his hands. "Shoot any chains attaching you to the ground. I'm going to fetch Ensign Marlow and his two companions then we're getting out of here in this airship."

Wright passed the rifle to his first officer, pointing at three chains running over the ship's railing. "That's not possible, sir. The galactic says the power is drained."

"No doubt the power is low, but no one runs their power out so completely that they use up the last little bit of it landing. I'll bet we have enough to get off this mountain before it runs out."

"Excellent. If you'll wait one moment, sir, I'll have some men to accompany you."

"The men stay on the airship, Captain." Wright opened his mouth to protest, but I talked over him. "That is an order."

"Aye aye, sir."

I vaulted the railing, drew my sword and charged toward the crowd around Chris and Forbose.

It only took a quick look at everyone crowding around the fight to verify that Chris and the two men chained to him were the only ones without weapons. That meant everyone except the three Mordanian airmen were excellent targets for Jade. I raised my sword and pointed it at the big knot of men and trogs ahead of me.

A blaster bolt flashed over my head, hitting a trog in the butt. He grabbed at his backside and fell, howling in pain. A few of the men standing next to him gave him curious glances. Just as they turned their attention back to the fight, another bolt struck. The man to the trog's left gaped as the bolt blew his arm off. More members of the crowd turned at the man's inarticulate cry. One of them spotted me—ten feet from the mob and just raising my sword—and shouted in alarm.

Boost!

I swung my sword in a wide arc, slashing deep cuts in five men across shoulders, chests, and arms. Blood—human red and trog blue—splattered the ground and others in the crowd. Two blaster rifles and three swords dropped to the ground as the wounded men fell away from me and out of my path. But that wasn't possible for the man directly between Chris and me.

The man tried backpedaling but the rest of the crowd blocked his way. A *third* blaster bolt hit the crowd to my left as the man before me raised his hands as if to ward off my next blow. I rammed my blade through his chest and up to the hilt. His eyes bulged as he folded around the sword through his gut. I caught one of his raised arms, holding the man up and using him as a battering ram against the crowd.

More blaster bolts hit the crowd. Between the screams of the men and the rain of rifle shots, the crowd finally figured out something was wrong. Heads swiveled and necks craned as they tried to see what was going on. The bloody blade protruding from the man I held nicked another man as he dove from my path and then it plunged deeply into the chest of a trog.

Finding myself in a widening clear spot, I stopped long enough to put a foot onto the chest of the man impaled on my blade. I pushed with my foot, pulled with my arm, and my sword slid free from the man and the trog. They fell in a heap before me.

I bounded over them and toward the last few men between me and the airmen. While I was in midair, someone from the anti-grav airship opened up with the blaster rifle. In the light spilling from the cave, my sword glistened red and blue. Splotches of human and trog blood covered my face and chest. With the flash of blaster bolts streaking past me, I like to think I truly appeared as the Hand of Death come reaping. The men and trogs before me must have agreed as they broke and scattered before I touched ground again.

For a second, Forbose stared at me in horrified fascination. Then Chris's fist struck the larger boy under the chin. Forbose's head snapped back, his eyes rolled up, and he slowly toppled backward.

From the cave came many voices and what sounded like the clatter of weapons. I shouted, "Men, get to the airship! It's time to go!"

Chris and the other two airmen caught sight of me for the first time. As their eyes widened, I realized they'd been so intent on the fight with Forbose the outcry behind them hadn't fully registered. Surprise rooting them in place, the trio stared in wonder at the confusion and carnage between them and the airship.

Men and trogs lay all around, bleeding and moaning, as blaster bolts blazed from the airship and Jade's position on the cliff. Meanwhile, I had a clear view of men and trogs massing in the cave.

Waving to catch the attention of my two gunners, I pointed into the cave mouth. Jade immediately shifted her aim and peppered the entrance to the cave with shots. The gunner on the airship followed suit and had the advantage of a better angle. His shots flashed into the massing crowd, sewing panic and confusion.

By this time, Chris and his friends were moving, running as fast as their chains allowed. That wasn't very fast, though, especially when the gathering force in the cave started returning fire. I took a second to look at the chain and was relieved to see it was of Aashlan origin instead of an unbreakable one from the Federation.

With Boost-backed strength and precision, I hacked at the smallest link in the chain. Tempered steel struck iron and the link shattered. That left Chris and an older airman still chained together. I struck again and all three men ran free.

The first airman reached the airship and the men onboard pulled him over the railing. At the same time, fatigue overwhelmed the older airman. He stumbled and would have fallen on his face had Chris not caught him. The Ensign staggered as he took the old man's weight and I feared both would fall.

I took the older crewman's other arm. "I've got him, Chris! Just concentrate on running." The young man released the other man, allowing me to lift him over one shoulder. Boosted muscles let me keep pace with the now-sprinting Ensign.

More blaster bolts struck all around us and I heard Captain Wright order his men to take cover behind the railing. All but the men assigned to help us climb onboard ducked out of sight. Blaster bolts scorched the side of the airship as Chris jumped to the waiting arms of the crewmen. As the young man's feet disappeared into the airship, I crouched and jumped. Even with the extra weight, I almost cleared the railing. My knees cracked painfully into the top of the railing and I toppled over into the airship. Safe for the moment, I dropped Boost.

I longed to sheath my sword, but only a fool puts a bloody blade into a sheath. Carefully pointing the blade down at the deck, I called, "Where are the airship's controls?"

A dozen arms pointed me aft. Heading that way, I called to the only crewman whose name I knew offhand. "Chris, we've got to get the gunner from the cliff on our way out. Go forward to lend a hand!"

"Aye aye, sir!"

I reached the airship controls and found myself staring at an odd combination of galactic high tech and Aashlan low tech.

Fortunately, I was one of only a handful of men on the planet who understood both technologies. I checked the system's power level and was gratified to find a ten percent charge. I flicked switches for each of the five repulsor plates and fed power to the engines at the same time.

"Captain Wright, send men below to feed the boiler. We've got just enough pressure to maneuver but not much more."

"Aye, Captain Rice," Wright said before issuing orders to his men.

More blaster bolts sizzled in the air as those in the cave fired at us. Worse, a few rifles were turned on Jade. She stopped shooting altogether as shots peppered her place on the cliff. The density of fire remained far lower than I'd feared but it only took one well-placed shot to ruin everything.

I twisted the power dial and the airship rose gracefully into the air. I cautiously engaged the engines and swung the ship toward Jade. "Are you ready, Chris?"

"I am, sir! Please hurry—the shots are hitting all around your man on the cliff!"

A REAL CLIFFHANGER

Jade

The blaster rifle felt odd in my hands. Far lighter than a crossbow, it was easy to move around and change aim. While waiting for David to do...whatever he was going to do, I practiced aiming at the crowd forming around Forbose and Chris. I got the hang of moving the rifle around quickly and found my attention drawn to the fistfight below.

I knew Forbose was good at fighting. He'd gotten into more than a few scraps back in Oshwindon and always came out on top. Some of my friends called him a bully, but Forbose always claimed the others started the fights and he ended them. Watching him pound on Chris, who was smaller and hampered by the chains, I realized just how willfully blind I'd been about Forbose. He grabbed Chris around the neck and hammered his fist into the smaller boy's ribs. Chris crouched and did his best to protect himself, all the while swinging away at Forbose. I was certain Forbose would claim he was simply defending himself and even insist Chris started the whole thing. For all I knew, he might even believe it.

But I didn't. Not any more. I saw Forbose's face. I saw the rage. I saw the bully. I saw the brute. And, in that second, I realized just how lucky I had been all those weeks ago out at the lake. If *this*

Forbose had surfaced, I felt certain he'd have forced himself on me. I realized, at long last, my mother had been right all along. I was ashamed how long it took me to see it.

And I fervently wished poor Chris wasn't paying the price for showing me the real Forbose.

Out of the corner of my eye, I saw someone leap from the strange airship. Before looking, I knew it could only be David. As he charged toward the crowd around Chris and Forbose, I took aim and started firing.

I aimed for a trog—and hit him right in the ass!

I shifted my aim to the man on the trog's left. The shot hit his upper arm and just blew the man's arm right off.

Forcing my mind away from that gross image, I kept firing into the crowd. Then David Boosted and I almost forgot what I was doing. Reading about David Boosting is one thing, watching David Boosting is something totally different. He was so fast! And so strong! And so amazing!

I forced myself to stop watching David and go back to shooting. That's why I saw Forbose freeze when he caught sight of David charging his way. That's why I saw Chris hit Forbose with an uppercut that lifted my totally ex-sort-of-boyfriend off the ground and laid him out.

"Chris, that was patchless!" I cried, knowing nobody heard me but wanting to shout it anyway.

Before I knew it, David had Chris and his companions free. They beat a hasty retreat for the airship, getting covering fire from me and someone on the ship. Seconds later, the airship slowly rose off the ground and its bow swung around toward me.

I kept firing at anyone who moved, only stopping when the blaster rifle's charge ran out. At least, I think that's what happened. The only things I knew about blasters came from adventure stories and who knew if those were accurate?

Then a blaster bolt struck the cliff's edge just below my position. Another followed. And another. Within seconds, blaster shots were flying all around me. Even though I had the ledge to protect me, the blaster bolts blew out chunks of rock each time they hit. Sharp rock shards flew all around me. By instinct, I rolled back and forth to stay clear of the shards—and any particularly well-placed blaster shots.

I tried keeping an eye on the airship, praying it would move a little faster or the people shooting at me would have their charges run out. Neither one of those happened.

The airship was only twenty feet from me when a bunch of blaster shots spattered all around me. Instinctively, I rolled away from the hot rock shards and other blaster bolts. This time, I completely screwed up and rolled over the edge of the ledge!

MY NAME IS JADE

Chris

When David ordered me to stand ready to help the shooter, I grabbed some rope and ran to the bow. The airship had little steam pressure, so we weren't moving very fast. That gave me plenty of time to tie the rope to a cleat on the bow and make sure there were no knots or tangles that might keep the rope from reaching the man on the ledge.

Then the villains below us rallied their defenses. Blaster shots flew all around us, many striking the airship's hull and almost as many striking all around David's man on the ledge. By the light of the blaster bolts, I watched him roll around the narrow ledge in an attempt to dodge the shots.

David called, "Are you ready, Chris?"

"I am, sir," I called. "Please hurry—the shots are landing all around your man on the cliff!"

The rolling man paused once, just long enough to look our way. I saw a wide-eyed face framed in long, blonde hair. It wasn't a man on the ledge at all. It was a girl! She rolled again, doing her best to get clear of the blaster shots and the rock shards flying all around her—and then the unthinkable happened.

The girl rolled too close to the edge. Already pock-marked from blaster bolts, the lip of the ledge gave way beneath her. With a cry, the girl fell. She caught the lip with fingers of her right hand, but her hold was precarious and couldn't last long.

I suddenly found myself swinging through the air, the rope clutched in my left hand. After that, everything happened faster than conscious thought. At the same time, everything happened in extreme slow motion. I know that doesn't make sense, but that's how I remember it.

I crossed the twenty feet separating us in a split second that lasted an entire year.

My bruised and battered left side crashed into the cliff face, sending waves of agony radiating through my body. Yet I felt no pain as I locked eyes with the dangling girl.

Her fingers were losing their grip as my right arm, moving as if through molasses, wrapped around her.

Renewed pain lanced through my body as the girl's fingers slipped off of the cliff and I took her full weight. With our faces no more than an inch apart, I felt nothing but wonder as I stared into the girl's eyes.

She wrapped her arms around me and buried her face against my neck. I felt more than heard her muffled, "Thank you!"

Blaster bolts flew all around us as we swung back toward the airship. Agony radiated from my left side. Yet this slender girl held all of my attention. Had time stopped right then, I would not have uttered a complaint.

But time did not stop. Hands grabbed the girl and me, pulling us over the airship's railing to safety. The men carried us to the center of the airship before gently putting us down. All the while, the girl arms remained wrapped tightly around my neck and her face tucked up against my neck. I kept my right arm around her, holding her close. Without conscious thought, I stroked her head with my left hand. Every movement hurt like hell, but I felt her panicked panting ease and her breathing slowly returning to normal.

"Well done, lad!" Captain Wright said, squatting next to us. "Miss, are you hurt?"

The girl shook her head and her arms tightened about my neck. "No, sir. Just frightened."

"No doubt," Captain Wright said, a smile flitting across his face. "What about you, Ensign Marlow? How are you?"

"Fine, sir."

"The hell he is!" the girl said, her tone vehement. "His left side got pounded in the fight that started all of this. I saw how much saving me hurt him. Chris, pull up your shirt so I can check your side."

I hesitated for a second, but Captain Wright's nod turned the girl's request into his order. Moving gingerly, I pulled up the left side of my shirt. It must have looked bad because the Captain drew breath in through closed teeth.

I know I should have been concerned about my side, but something else held my attention. "How do you know my name, miss?"

"David told me," she said, gently probing my injured side. "Thank you, again, for saving my life."

"You're most welcome, miss," I replied.

She smiled at me, or perhaps at my formal tone. Her smile was spellbinding. She was entrancing. I suddenly realized my right arm was still wrapped around her. I began pulling my arm back but the girl caught my hand and held it in place. I tightened my arm, smiling back at this girl who so literally fell into my life. And I found myself fervently praying my arm would always have a place around her waist.

Her smile widened. "My name is Jade."

FRATERNIZATION AND FIGHTING

David

My heart leapt into my throat as I watched Jade's hands flail desperately for a handhold. The fingers of the girl's right hand caught the lip of the ledge she'd been laying on and stopped her fall. The rest of her body swung down and around her tenuous grip. Her feet smacked into the ladder, loosening her grip and sending her swinging back in the other direction just before her left hand could grab the ladder.

All of this took but a split second and my cry of horror was still forming when Chris took action. With a ship's line clutched in his left hand, the Ensign dove over the railing, swinging toward Jade like some kind of jungle lord. Chris came up beside the dangling girl, crashing into the cliff with his wounded left side. Even in the dim light, the pain was evident on Chris's face. Ignoring it, the boy wrapped his free arm around Jade, pulling her close against him just as her fingertips lost their grip on the ledge!

Both teenagers gave muffled cries—Jade, I assume, in relief and Chris, obviously, in pain as his injured side took the full weight of another person. Then the pair swung away from the cliff, the long arc bringing them back to the airship and almost to the height of the railing.

Captain Wright, shouting orders to his crew from the second

Jade rolled off the cliff's edge, had his crew well positioned. Half a dozen men leaned far over the edge of the airship, their own weight anchored by crew mates holding onto their legs. The airmen caught the rope, the girl, and the Ensign. Those holding onto the airmen pulled them all over the railing to safety.

All the while, blaster bolts lit the cliff face as they streaked at the underside of the airship. The smell of smoke rose from the hull as the dry wood smoldered and started burning.

I twisted the repulser power knob to one hundred percent lift. The rapid ascent caught the crew by surprise, knocking many of them off their feet and pressing down on all of us.

"Captain Wright, the bottom of the hull is on fire!" I shouted over the din of blaster shots and shouting men. "Prepare to abandon ship once we reach the top of the cliff!"

Wright skipped an acknowledgment of my order and went straight to issuing his own orders. He sent men below to scrounge anything useful they could find—from food and water to weapons. Crewmen scattered to do their captain's bidding.

"Someone find the medical kit, too!" Jade's voice cut through the hubbub on the deck, no doubt a skill she learned working on the *Wind Dancer*. "Chris is hurt!"

I spent almost an entire second wondering how the girl knew the Ensign's name before remembering I'd all but shouted it myself when I spotted Chris while on the ledge with Jade.

"You heard the young lady!" Wright added his authority to Jade's demand. "And I want two crewmen to assist Ensign Marlow's debarkation when we land!"

The airship climbed above the top edge of the cliff and I fed what power the steam engines had into the propellers. The density of blaster fire dropped to only a handful of shots and most of them replaced with the sound of feet running across the desert floor. I assumed Thor ordered a team to ascend the ladders, hoping to have troops hot on our trail as we ran from his mountain. Meanwhile, he'd send other troops to block our escape. It's a basic pincer maneuver and just the sort of thing a mind untrained in military tactics selects.

Alas for Thor, I had a big surprise in mind for him.

Once the airship had solid ground beneath it, I brought it down quickly and Mordanian airmen hopped off the airship. Under Jade's watchful eye, two men carefully lowered Chris to other men waiting below to catch him. One of the airmen then offered a hand to Jade, who ignored it and jumped lithely down next to Chris.

Once all were clear of the ship, I vaulted over the railing to land next to Captain Wright. "Our adversary is sending men up the cliff after us, Captain. I suggest we discourage this pursuit."

"I concur wholeheartedly, sir, but they have men providing covering fire. If we try to shoot over the edge of the cliff, our men will be in danger of being shot in return."

"Oh, we're not going to waste time and risk lives shooting at them, Captain." I jerked a thumb over my shoulder at the anti-grav airship. "I think we should give them back their airship."

A feral grin spread over the Captain's face. "Men, form up around this airship and let's push it over the cliff!"

Airmen ran to positions all around the airship. I saw Chris struggling to join his crew and Jade struggling to keep him from doing just that.

"Ensign Marlow," I said, stepping over to the reclining boy, "as you were."

"But sir-" Chris protested.

"You are in no condition to push an airship, Ensign," I said.

"That's what *I* told him," Jade huffed.

"She's right, Chris," I said. "In fact, I'm officially putting you under her orders until further notice."

"But she's a civilian, sir!"

"Good point, Ensign." I smiled at Jade. "How would you like to be a medic in the Mordanian Navy? Temporarily, of course. Only until we can return you to your father."

"If it'll help keep Chris from killing himself, I'm all for it," Jade replied.

"Welcome to the Navy, young lady." I turned back to Chris. "Satisfied?"

"Um, I guess." Chris allowed Jade to push him prone again.

During our short conversation, the girl had somehow managed to position herself so Chris's head ended up in her lap. I tried to think what Callan—who is always ready and willing to encourage romance—would say at this moment.

"Jade, Chris is under your orders but not part of your chain of command."

From the look on Chris's face, he understood what I meant immediately. Jade's face screwed up in puzzlement and she asked, "Huh?"

"Fraternization is allowed," I said.

I thought Jade blushed, but it was dark and I couldn't be certain. But when I looked at the two a few seconds later, Jade and Chris had their heads close together. The girl, at least, looked prepared to explore the concept of fraternization. I thought the young Ensign appeared quite interested, as well, but then Captain Wright's voice called out orders to push.

Along with the rest of the airmen, I put my shoulder against the hull and shoved. For once, the loose stones that covered most of the mountain worked in our favor. I'd left a small amount of power running to the repulser plates. It wasn't nearly enough to keep the ship in the air, but it did reduce the weight somewhat.

It took three good shoves before the airship slid a few inches. Once it moved the first time, it was easier to move a second time. When it moved the third time, it didn't stop. The crew kept pushing until the stern, with the heavy boiler and most of the anti-grav machinery, overbalanced and the entire airship tipped up and plunged over the edge of the cliff.

Cries of fear rose from the men ascending the ladders then cut off suddenly. A second later, the airship crashed to the ground far below. With a satisfying boom, the boiler blew. The fearful cries turned to agonized screams as the explosion sent scalding-hot steam washing over everyone around and above it.

Captain Wright appeared before me. "The ladders have been sheared off the cliff, sir, along with our pursuers."

"Please give my compliments to the crew for a job well done, Captain," I said. "Gather the men and supplies. We've got a long march ahead of us and I expect Thor will prove unwilling to simply let us walk away."

"Aye sir," Wright replied. His eyes cut to his Ensign and Jade, their cheeks touching though not actively kissing at the moment. "And, um, what about Ensign Marlow and the young lady?"

"She's officially our medic for right now and I've put the Ensign under her orders."

Wright smiled. "It appears he's complying fully. I'll tell the men that the first man to tease either of them will answer to you."

"Go one better, Captain. Tell the crew they'll answer to my wife."

Wright laughed. "Yes, that threat will keep them in line."

"Have the men form up behind me. We leave as soon as they're ready."

To no one's surprise, Jade helped Chris to his feet and stayed at his side. Wright made sure an airman was nearby to offer help if Chris needed it, though Jade was supporting him well enough for the moment. The men were ready in less than a minute.

With only the light from the planetary ring to illuminate our path, we started the long march away from Thor's base.

As the line of airmen got underway, I fell in beside Chris and Jade. The girl had Chris's right arm draped over her shoulder, providing support while staying away from his injured ribs. Life on an airship gave Jade strength beyond that of an average sixteen-year-old girl, but Chris was both taller and heavier than she was. Jade wore a determined expression and I thought she'd rather collapse with exhaustion than let down the boy who rescued her from the cliff. Chris's face was equally set and I was sure he'd rather die than show weakness before the pretty blonde.

"Listen up you two." Chris and Jade looked at me. "Speed is of the utmost importance right now. The longer it takes us to get off this mountain, the greater the chance we'll have to fight our way off of it. In other words, this is *not* the time to try to be an iron-man, Chris. You took a hell of a beating fighting Forbose."

Chris interrupted, "How do you know that guy's name? Is he from one of the other Navy ships?"

"No," Jade answered. "I...know him. Or at least thought I knew him."

"Anyway," I took back control of the conversation, "if you're having trouble keeping up with the rest of us, you must tell Captain Wright or me. Your injuries were honorably earned in the service of your country. The men will want to help you. Is that clear?"

"Yes, sir."

Jade added, "Don't worry. If he gets stubborn, *I'll* call you."

"That's nothing less than I'd expect from our medic." I smiled briefly at the girl before hardening my gaze. "But what I said to Chris applies equally to you, Jade."

"Huh?"

"Don't let your desire to help Chris keep you from asking for help supporting Chris. You're going to have to switch out with some of the men eventually. Do that as soon as you feel tired. Chris doesn't want you wearing yourself out any more than you want him doing it."

Jade nodded. "Okay."

Chris grinned. "And if *she* gets stubborn, I'll call you."

I rejoined Captain Wright at the front of the column. I told him about my instructions to Chris and Jade, then asked, "How are the men set for weapons?"

Wright grimaced. "Rather poorly, sir. The young lady's blaster rifle is out of...whatever the thing shoots. There were no swords on board that airship, of course. We've mostly got makeshift clubs."

"Did the trogs plunder the wreck of the *Vanguard* after they captured you?"

"Not that I saw. After all, why take swords and crossbows when you've already got blaster rifles?"

"Okay, we'll go back to the wreck and arm ourselves as best we can," I said, "Our enemies have better weapons, but they can only fire so many times before running out of power."

"I don't suppose you can be more specific than that, sir?" Wright asked.

"A Federation-manufactured blaster has approximately fifty shots per power pack." Wright winced at the answer and I added, "But these blasters are hand-made from spare parts. The work is very clever, I'll grant you, but I doubt their batteries are up to galactic standards. The rifles are probably less efficient with their energy usage, too."

"I wish your reassurances used fewer words like 'doubt' and 'probably,' sir."

"Me, too, Captain." I was quiet for a few seconds as I considered the trail ahead of us. "Do you have a couple of particularly stealthy men in the crew? I'd like to send some scouts ahead of us."

Wright selected Jon, a reformed thief, and Horst, a hunter, sending them on their way after I told them where to find the cave that led into the base. All the while, we kept the men moving as quickly as possible. In passing, I noted Jade summoning an airman to take her place supporting Chris. Free to roam, Jade took the chance to check up on other wounded men. She instructed two to come to her at the next rest stop for a change of bandages, receiving a respectful "Yes, ma'am" in reply both times.

During that next rest stop, one of our scouts returned bearing a wide grin and another blaster rifle. The two scouts found Frank and Van napping by the trail, tied and gagged the pair of idiots with their own clothing, and split up. Jon returned with one of the rifles while the hunter covered the cave exit.

"The trail is clear right now, sir. With that rifle, Horst can probably hold that cave exit long enough for us to get past it," the former thief reported. "I'd like permission to run ahead with one of the rifles and help him hold the trail."

At my nod, Jon turned and ran down back the way he'd come.

Once Jade finished changing bandages, we got everyone up and moving double-time after Jon.

For once, fortune smiled on us. We passed the cave without incident, picking up Jon and Horst along the way. The scouts had exchanged a little fire with trogs and men exiting the cave. I don't know what ran through Thor's mind, but he didn't waste lives trying to break past our men. No doubt there was another exit somewhere within a mile of the cave. I expected we still had a fight coming, I just hoped it would happen on terrain of our choosing.

Half an hour later, we reached the wreck of the *Vanguard* and the men immediately hunted up swords for everyone. By a stroke of luck, a dozen crossbows escaped the fires. Our good mood lasted all of ten minutes.

"Men and trogs are coming!" one of our lookouts called.

Finding myself strangely relieved that the waiting was over, I called, "How many of them did Thor send against us?"

"At a guess, sir, I'd say all of them."

I bounded to the top of a piece of wrecked hull and looked at the mountain. At least five hundred men and trogs advanced on us.

I looked from the wide line of approaching men and trogs to my own men gathered around the wreck of the *Vanguard*. A dozen crossbows and perhaps a hundred swords against four hundred swords and another hundred blaster rifles? It was quite literally bows and arrows against the lightning—only those wielding the lightning also had numbers on their side.

Speaking quietly, so only I could hear him, Captain Wright said, "We're outmanned *and* outgunned. These are brave men, sir, who will fight for you to the last man. But unless something unexpected happens, I do not see a happy outcome for us."

"I won't ask that of them, Captain, but I also won't just give up without some attempt at a fight."

"I expected no less, sir." Wright inclined his head toward the men. "Perhaps you'd care to say a few words to the men before all hell breaks loose?"

Nodding, I let my gaze wander over the gathered men while gathering my thoughts.

"Give me your attention, men!" Silence fell as I called out. "By now you've heard the opposing force outnumbers us five to one. If the enemy was armed as we are, I'd take those odds all day, any day. But the enemy is not armed as we are. They have as many blaster rifles as we have men. I don't know how we can defend against those. If—"

"Captain Rice, sir?" a young voice called from the crowd.

"Do not interrupt your commanding officer, Ensign Marlow!" Wright snapped.

"No, Captain, it's okay," I said. "I was about to ask for suggestions. Chris, do you have an idea?"

"I think so, sir. Jade told me about the dust cloud you created with her family's airship." The girl stood to Chris's left, her arm hooked through his. "If what her father told her is right, the dust sort of absorbed the blaster shots."

"That's right, Ensign, and if we had a working engine I'd be all for trying it again." I pointed to the scattered remains of the *Vanguard's* engines. "Unfortunately, we don't."

"I realize that, sir, but we *do* have buckets, a lot of men, and plenty of dust and sand. Couldn't two or three bucket brigades throw up enough dust to do the job?"

I glanced over my shoulder. The advancing horde was still half a mile away and appeared content with their steady march forward. Looking back at Chris, I said, "It's an interesting idea, Chris, but there's no way we could throw up enough dust to protect an entire line of battle."

"But we don't need to protect the entire line, sir," Chris said. "We just need to protect a dozen crossbowmen. If our best marksmen can shoot unhindered, maybe they can thin out the men with blaster rifles and make those men waste shots firing back."

I stared at Chris for a moment, noting the big grin worn by Jade. Turning to Captain Wright, I said, "Select your dozen best marksmen. Have the rest of your men form into four bucket brigades and start filling buckets with dust."

Wright immediately pointed out a dozen men, most of whom already had crossbows. Those men fell into technical discussions about range and wind and volley firing. I left them to it and made my way over to Chris and Jade.

I handed our lone blaster rifle to the girl. "You're familiar enough with these that I want you handling it. Don't try shooting through the dust, obviously."

"Of *course* not." Jade rolled her eyes but surprised me by adding, "Sir."

"That was a good idea, Chris," I said to the Ensign. "Let's pray it works."

"It was your idea, sir, not mine. Not originally." Chris smiled at the girl next to him. "Besides, Jade is the one who deserves the real credit."

"Don't listen to him, David, um sir," Jade said. "I just said it was too bad we didn't have a way to do that here. Chris did the rest."

"So noted, Jade," I replied. "Chris, you're not in any condition to take part in the bucket brigade, so I want you to stay with Jade. If the situation gets too dangerous, get her out of here. Is that clear?"

Chris nodded.

"And if Chris says it's time to go, you go with him, Jade." I gave her a mock glare. "No sneaking off to look for lost sort-of boyfriends and no arguing. Right?"

"Right," Jade answered.

"And if either of you comes up with any other ideas for defending ourselves, inform me immediately."

As I turned away, Chris asked Jade, "Wait, that Forbose guy was your boyfriend?"

"Sort of. Maybe," Jade responded. "But not anymore after what he did to you!"

The rest of the teenagers' conversation faded into the background as Captain Wright and I inspected the bucket brigades and the firing positions chosen by the crossbowmen. Satisfied with the preparations, we watched the approaching line and waited.

"You know, if they had anyone with even rudimentary military instincts, they'd surround us before attacking," Captain Wright noted.

"Let us thank God for small favors, Captain."

He nodded and it was as if that was the signal our enemies had been waiting for. They broke into a trot and a few of the ones armed with blaster rifles took shots. None of those shots came close and the rest of Thor's men held their fire as the line closed in on us.

Then a roar rose from five hundred throats and Thor's men charged.

As more and more of Thor's men and trogs joined the charge, the sound of feet pounding on the desert quickly grew from a series of staccato thumps into a constant roll of thunder. Voices rose in defiance, calling for revenge and destruction. Random blaster shots flashed through the air. Some of them blasted chunks from the remains of the *Vanguard*, others missed entirely, blazing into the dawn.

"When you're ready, Captain Wright," I said, gauging the distance between the charging horde and our crossbowmen.

"Bucket brigades," the Captain barked, "begin!"

Three men threw buckets full of sand and dust into the air before the hidden crossbowmen. On the backswing, they tossed the buckets to the ground and then caught the next bucket from the man behind them. All along the line, men, pushed buckets forward then reached back to take another bucket. Much of the sand and dirt settled quickly to the ground, but the air before us also filled with whirling particles of dust.

"Crossbowman, take position!" At Captain Wright's command, the dozen men bearing crossbows scrambled to the top of the *Vanguard's* hull. Six took a knee while the other six stood right behind them. "Pick your targets and fire when ready!"

The first crossbow snapped, then another and another after

that. Two hundred yards away, a man stumbled and fell. A second and third man fell as well. Within seconds, the crossbows clicked and thrummed almost without pause as each man fired, reloaded, aimed, and fired again. With such a massive target before them, every shot hit someone—perhaps it was just an arm or leg hit, though many times the bolts buried themselves into chests or heads.

Watching as closely as the gray light allowed, I marveled how many of those hit carried blaster rifles. I saw men trampled as they went down ahead of their charging fellows and took grim satisfaction when I saw blaster rifles mangled and broken underfoot.

Meanwhile, a few of the riflemen took time to stop and aim more carefully. Most of those shots were also off-target. The few that were on-target dissipated and lost power in the swirling cloud of dust. A very few shots still managed to get through and hit two men. One took a nasty burn to the shoulder and the other a scorch on the forearm. Both men waved away the medic, insisting they were fine, and continued firing.

After what seemed like hours of charging, the men and trogs drew too close to maintain our position atop the hull. Everyone retreated to the ground and then moved into our positions within the hull itself. The holes in the sides served as perfect choke points, so we concentrated our men defending those positions. Seconds after everyone was in place, the mass of men and trogs swarmed around the remains of the *Vanguard* and the real battle began in earnest.

Captain Wright and I ran back and forth through the wrecked airship's passageways, directing reinforcements to areas most hard-pressed, helping pull wounded men away from the front line, and throwing ourselves into weakening lines and plugging breaches until help could arrive. Yells and cries and the clash of weapons drowned all but the loudest shout, forcing us to rely on hand signals to convey orders. In the close quarters, the stench of sweat and blood and fear permeated everything.

Jade surprised me by popping up all around the ship, taking a couple of shots with the blaster rifle to drive the attackers back for a few seconds, then dashing off to some other part of the ship to do the same. Then someone grabbed a second blaster rifle from a downed attacker and passed it into Chris's hands. He followed Jade's lead, with both teenagers concentrating on opposing riflemen. Within a few minutes, we had gathered a dozen more blaster rifles and put them in the hands of those too wounded for hand-to-hand fighting but fully capable of pulling a trigger.

Our men poured shot after shot past our front lines and into the packed men and trogs pushing and shoving to break through. Those at the front recoiled, only to be pushed back into the fight by those behind them. Then some of the shots scored hits deeper into the mass of bodies and those at the back realized their danger. The men and trogs on the outside of the horde backed away and then turned and ran. As each layer of attackers realized that retreat lay open to them, they broke off pushing and took to their heels.

According to my implant, thirty-six long minutes passed between our retreat inside the *Vanguard* and our attackers' retreat.

A ragged cheer rose from our men when the last of the enemy vanished from our sight.

"Well done, Mr. Rice," Thor's amplified voice called from well away from the *Vanguard*. "Once again, you found a clever use for the dirt and dust of this backward planet and somehow managed to find a way to rout my much larger and much better-equipped army. But I am tired of dealing with you and your little band. You have one minute in which to throw down your arms and surrender to my army."

"And if I refuse?" I yelled, confident Thor could hear me.

"Then I'll set fire to that hulk you're hiding in and burn you all alive."

BACK IN THE HUNT

Callan

The *Tercel*, Mordan's mighty tammar of the skies, huddled like a frightened rabbit in the lee of the rocky projection. The windstorm raged about us, sweeping rocks and sand and dust ahead of it. The storm's detritus fell upon us, scouring the exposed deck and hull of the *Tercel*, and what wind found its way around the alcove rocked the mighty airship as easily as a mother rocks her newborn babe.

I sat below deck, with most of the crew packed around me. Hand-picked crewman remained on deck, tied to their stations with safety lines and ready to cut the envelope free if the wind changed direction and brought its full strength to bear on us again. If I understood the concept of the storm machine properly, the wind could only change directions if the machine moved. Captain Jorson was unwilling to gamble my life and the lives of his crew on my meager understanding of galactic technology and I couldn't fault the man for that.

The youngest members of the crew—from ship's boys of nine or ten years to the junior ensigns, who were all of twelve or thirteen—were gathered around me. Captain Jorson placed the lot of us in the most protected position below deck. Sweat ran freely down our faces as heat gathered in the enclosed space. Wide, young eyes darted all around the inside of the airship, drawn to every creak and crack of the hull. The ensigns strove to emulate the outward calm of their superior officers, but they were simply too young to pull it off.

"I suppose all of you fine young men have heard all about David's—Captain Rice's—arrival on Aashla?" I asked.

The ship's boys nodded shyly while a chorus of "Yes, Your Highness" rose from the ensigns. One added, "When I was little, I heard Megan the Bard—um, Mrs. Bane—sing *The Scout and the Princess* once."

The other boys cast envious looks at the Ensign, prompting me to say, "Megan will be back on Aashla in a few months. I'll see if I can arrange a concert for the *Tercel's* crew. But have you ever heard the story from someone who was actually there?"

Nine boys shook their heads in unison, eyes widening in interest rather than fear.

"Rob, the captain of my guard, and I stood by ourselves against at least two dozen trogs. I was certain the end was upon us. That's when *he* arrived..."

Small mouths hung open in wonder as I wove the tale I knew so well. It was my son's favorite bedtime story, after all. Beyond the ensigns and ship's boys, the older crew slowly fell silent, drawn into the story as well. I raised my voice as more and more men cupped hands around ears in an effort to hear me over the wind. I lost myself in the telling and it was only when Captain Jorson bellowed for all hands on deck that I realized the storm was over.

As the crew scrambled to their feet, one of the ship's boys looked up at me and solemnly said, "Don't you worry none, Your Highness! We ain't gonna let nothing happen to Captain Rice!"

With equal solemnity, I nodded to the boy. "I have complete faith in the *Tercel* and her crew."

Those around me passed my words to those farther away, who passed them on until the whole crew knew. As I emerged from the hold onto the blessedly cool deck, Captain Jorson met me with a formal salute. All around us, the crew worked with steady speed to ready the airship for flight.

"The crew is truly inspired, both by your story and your faith in them."

"They are Mordanian airmen, Captain Jorson," I said as if that explained everything. To members of the Mordanian Navy, it *did* explain everything.

"Exactly so, Your Highness!"

Less than five minutes after I emerged onto the deck, the *Tercel* rose into the predawn sky. The mighty steam engines came to life and the airship's propellers churned the air. *Tercel* gathered speed, reaching its normal cruising speed within twenty minutes—and still she kept accelerating.

"Keep the pressure up, lads!" exhorted the airship's engineer from the stern. "It's better for us to show up early and Captain Rice not need our help than to show up late and find him desperate for it!"

"Mister Carson," Jorson called to the engineer, "can the engines take much more of this?"

"Aye, sir! They're *my* engines!" Indignation evident in both his tone and posture, Mister Carson added, "May I also remind the Captain that the engines are highly sensitive and likely to take affront if they hear you questioning them?"

"You may assure them it was only concern for their wellbeing that prompted my question, Mister Carson." Captain Jorson turned away from the engineer and caught sight of my raised eyebrows. "Mister Carson is eccentric, but he is also the best engineer in the fleet."

As the airship approached speeds even my good friend and pilot Nist would consider acceptable, I found myself forced to concur with Captain Jorson's assessment. The sun peeked over the distant horizon and quickly spread the bright light of dawn over the desert before us.

I was concentrating on the mountains ahead of us, sure the galactics' mountain base must be near, when the lookout shouted, "Sir, there's fighting around the wreck of the *Vanguard*!"

A CRAFTY CHALLENGE

David

My gaze swept over the men gathered in *Vanguard's* largest hold. Hard eyes looked back from faces covered with blood and sweat and grime. Each face wore a grim, resolute smile. Men too wounded to stand on their own were supported by comrades. Front and center, unconsciously holding hands, Jade and Chris watched me with the same resolution as the rest.

I turned to the man standing next to me. "Captain Wright, you heard our opponent's demand. Should we accede to it?"

"Sir, the finest crew of the finest ship to ever sail the skies of Aashla stands before you," Wright said. "Men like these are destined for greatness—and you don't achieve greatness by giving up!"

A ragged cheer rose from the men. I held my hands up and silence fell immediately.

"Ensign Marlow?" I asked.

Surprised to hear his name called, Chris released Jade's hand and snapped to attention. I returned his salute before saying, "At ease, Ensign."

I looked back and forth between the two teenagers. "I have a particularly tough set of orders for you, Ensign. I want you to lead Jade, the other three ensigns, and the four ship's boys to safety."

"You want me to abandon my ship and my crew in their most desperate hour, sir?" Surprise and consternation filled Chris's voice.

"I want you to save the youngest and most vulnerable members of this crew. I want you to carry on in memory of the *Vanguard*. I want her story told far and wide. And, should this be the end for those of us who stay, I want you to offer comfort to the families of the crew—from the parents of the lowest ranked airman to Her Royal Highness, Princess Callan." I placed a hand on the young Ensign's shoulder. "I told you my orders were particularly tough. Are you up to it?"

"Aye, aye, sir!" Chris snapped.

All in all, it was a truly moving moment. One filled with manly stoicism. Every man present swelled with pride and honor. The teenage girl present was less impressed.

Her green eyes wide in what I soon recognized was incredulity, Jade said, "Wow, you guys really are ready to die and you're feeling pretty damned pleased with yourselves about the whole thing. Far be it from me to get in the way of your mad charge toward the grave, but could I offer a suggestion first?"

All around the hold, men turned affronted glares on the girl. Next to me, I sensed Captain Wright drawing himself up to issue a stern rebuke. I hurried to speak first.

"If you have a better idea, Jade, I will be most happy to hear it."

"Why don't you just challenge this Thor guy to a duel for leadership of the army?" she asked.

I furrowed my brow, puzzled. "You know as well as I do that he won't accept the challenge. It won't even buy us an extra minute, so what would be the point?"

Jade actually rolled her eyes at my question. "Did you pay any attention to the army you're fighting? At least half of them are trogs."

Comprehension dawned on me, though Chris responded first. "Of course! If he refuses, the trogs will see him as a coward and abandon him! And if he fights, Captain Rice will kill him! That's brilliant!"

His face shining with excitement, Chris wrapped his arms around Jade and kissed her. Surprised, Jade stiffened for a second before settling into the kiss. Hoots and hollers from the crew suddenly got through to the young couple. Blushing furiously, they broke apart, eyes downcast.

"My deepest apologies, sir," Chris said. "I don't know what came over me."

At a glance from Wright, I let him respond to his Ensign. "You *should* apologize, Ensign Marlow. If *I* were in your place, I'd kiss the young lady a second time!"

The crew laughed as Chris and Jade stared at Wright in surprise. From somewhere in the crowd, a voice called, "Don't just stand there gawking, lad! Vanguards never shirk their duty!"

I waited a few seconds for the embarrassed pair to finish a much more awkward kiss.

"Ensign Marlow, while our plans have changed, your orders have not. I still believe this will come to a fight and, now that we've got the enemy fixated on those of us inside the *Vanguard*, I want our youngest crew members away from here."

"Aye, sir," Chris responded. "With your permission, I'll gather my charges."

When I nodded, Chris and Jade went through the various holds. They returned a minute later, trailed by the ensigns and ship's boys.

"Stay low, keep the *Vanguard* between you and Thor's little army, and don't stop for anything except a direct order from a superior officer," I said. "Do you have any questions?"

"No, sir."

"Good. Take two of the blaster rifles and swords for you and the other ensigns. Leave as soon as I call out to Thor and draw their attention to me."

With that, I left the broken hull and climbed atop it. Wright came with me as Chris and the other youngsters waited for my challenge.

"Do you have any idea why this Thor fellow pulled all his men back to him?" Wright asked. "A smart commander would have kept us encircled."

"We already know Thor isn't a smart commander. He's a brilliant technician, I'll grant you, and probably assumes brilliance in one area means he's brilliant at everything else." I stared across the quarter mile of open ground to Thor's army, trying to pick him out of the crowd. He wasn't anywhere near the front. "I also suspect he's afraid I'll Boost, somehow cross a quarter of a mile before anyone reacts, and kill him. So he surrounds himself with sword fodder."

"Coward," Wright muttered.

Instead of responding, I raised my voice and yelled, "Thor, can you hear me?"

From somewhere within the mass of men and trogs, a voice responded, "Yes. Are you ready to surrender?"

"Not in the least," I called. "I challenge you to trial by combat for leadership of your army!"

Amplified laughter rang out in response to my challenge. When Thor managed to control his mirth enough to talk, he did so in galactic basic. Derision dripping from every syllable, he said, "Can you truly be that stupid, Rice? Have you spent so much time reading the public accounts of your so-called adventures that you've begun to believe them?"

"I have little interest in reading some writer's interpretation of my life." After my initial response in galactic basic, I switched to Mordanian. "Should I assume you are refusing my challenge?"

Thor stuck to gal base, giving me the impression none of his followers spoke the language. "I am under no illusions concerning my prowess as a fighter, Rice. I'm far too intelligent to think I would stand a chance against you in a fight. You, on the other hand, have bought into this planet's ridiculous concepts of manhood. You were raised in the Terran Federation—surely you understand all of this talk of honor and duty is nothing more than the prattle of an ignorant populace."

"Perhaps it is *you* who led a sheltered life in the Federation, Thor." I stuck to Mordanian, trying to make sure the gist of Thor's words got through to the trogs around him. After my brief run-in with the trogs at the top of the mountain, I felt safe assuming some of them understood me. "I learned of honor and duty from a young age and felt right at home in the Scout Academy."

Thor snorted at that. "I rest my case. I must admit this has been amusing, Rice, but now it's time for you to surrender or die in a pointless display of that honor you hold so dear."

"I had to try, Thor," I called back. "For the record, would you please respond to my challenge in Mordanian?"

Thor heaved an amplified sigh and switched languages. "Very well, Rice. Let it be known that I decline your challenge to a duel."

I watched the trogs on the edges of Thor's mass of followers, waiting for them to respond to Thor's refusal. I was still looking for movement from the trogs when Wright caught my arm.

Pointing to the left side of the mass before us, the Captain said, "There, sir!"

I looked where he pointed and relief flooded through me. A small band of trogs broke away from the men around them and jogged back toward the mountain. Then another group of trogs broke from the crowd's fringe. Then it became evident the trogs deeper inside the crowd were pushing their way through the men.

Someone near Thor spoke, his words amplified just as Thor's had been. "Sir, the trogs are leaving!"

"I can see that!" Thor snapped. "Find out why."

"They won't follow you anymore, Thor," I called.

"How do you know that, Rice?"

I admit taking extreme pleasure from my answer. "Surely a man of your vast intellect can figure it out."

"Damn you, Rice, did you work some stupid code phrases into your words?" Anger warred with confusion in Thor's voice.

"Not at all, Thor. In fact, the trogs aren't leaving because of anything *I* said." A triumphant note crept into my voice. "They're leaving because you refused my challenge."

"That's absurd," Thor scoffed. "Only an idiot would have accepted your challenge! I cannot believe any being wishes to follow an idiot."

"Didn't you bother to study up on the trogs before you decided to come here and lead them in a great revolt against humanity?"

"I skimmed it, along with the obviously fictional story of David Rice, the great hero of Aashla," Thor said. "My intellectual peers and I dismissed the propaganda spewed by the hand-picked so-called scientists you and the other oppressors allowed on this planet. Any child could recognize your attempts at myth-making."

"At the risk of sounding trite, Thor, I think you're just too damned smart for your own good!" The men gathered around me laughed as I continued, "I suspect you're right, trogs probably don't want to follow idiots. But I *know* they refuse to follow cowards. When you refused my challenge, you showed your cowardice. That was pretty stupid, don't you think?"

"We still outnumber you by more than two-to-one, Rice, and you're only protection is a hulk of wood!" Thor raged. "Men, forget my orders to take prisoners. Burn the wreck and slaughter them all!"

With a bloodthirsty yell, the men still under Thor's command charged.

TOO LATE

Callan

At the lookout's call, I rushed to the bow of the *Tercel*, joining Captain Jorson and his first officer. "Can you see anything of this battle, Captain?"

"Yes, Your Highness, and what I can see is strange to say the least!" Jorson replied. "There are three groups out there, not the two I expected."

"May I borrow a spyglass and see for myself?" I asked.

The first officer offered his glass to me. "I'd be honored, Princess Callan."

"Thank you, Lieutenant..." I ducked my head in embarrassment. "I beg your pardon, but I don't know your name."

The man saluted. "James Tucker at your service, Your Highness."

"Thank you, Lieutenant Tucker," I said, raising the spyglass to my eye.

It took me a moment to find the wreck of the *Vanguard* and bring it into focus, but my heart leapt at the sight before me. David stood atop the broken hull with Captain Wright next to him. Seventy or eighty of the airship's crew crouched just behind the keel. A hundred yards away, close to two hundred men charged across the desert toward them. Just as many trogs jogged slowly away from the impending battle. And in between the two groups stood a lone man, his head swiveling back and forth between the charging men and the retreating trogs.

"Well, I see my husband managed to put himself right in the middle of another battle," I said, lowering the glass. "He'd better enjoy it because we have one thing to do before we can help him."

"We do, Your Highness?" Jorson asked.

"Most definitely, Captain. Do you see the man standing between the charging men and the retreating trogs? I want him. Take him alive if you can. Kill him if you can't."

"You think he's the ringleader?" the Captain asked.

"Most definitely. He's attempting to lead this battle from the rear, which isn't the way we do things here on Aashla. And just look at the way he's dressed—not even the most ridiculous court jester would wear such clothing in public." Jorson and Tucker exchanged mystified glances at my comment. I patted both men on the arm. "Surely you're willing to accept a woman's word when it comes to fashion, gentlemen?"

"Ah, yes, most definitely, Your Highness. I freely admit my wife must exercise the fashionable eye for both of us. I am hopelessly blind in such matters." Jorson then pointed toward the retreating trogs. "But I doubt Thor's ignorance of Aashlan fashion repulsed the trogs. Begging Her Highness's pardon for my language, but I'll be damned if I can figure out why they're leaving."

"I heard worse language from my guards when I still slept in the palace nursery, Captain. No pardon is required. As for the trogs, I expect David challenged Thor to a duel and Thor refused," I said. "I just wonder if David thought of it himself. Once he's decided fighting is the only way out of a situation, he tends toward tunnel vision."

Jorson nodded, "That would explain things. With your permission, Your Highness, Lieutenant Tucker and I will give the orders to snatch Thor and then go to your husband's aid."

"Of course, Captain. Though if you could spare a few seconds to have a speaking trumpet brought to me, I'd appreciate it."

"Certainly. I'm sure the men would appreciate a word from you before heading into battle."

"Which I'll be delighted to give, Captain, though I think they'll appreciate allies even more." The two officers looked at me blankly, so I pointed at the trogs. "They aren't willing to follow Thor any longer, but perhaps they'll follow Lady Death in defense of the Hand of Death."

Comprehension dawned on the two men when they heard the trogs' nickname for David and me. Tucker grinned broadly, "Just retribution, if ever I heard it, Your Highness!"

I turned back toward the fight, raising Tucker's glass to my eye. As orders rang out behind me, the mass of charging men swarmed up the side of the *Vanguard's* broken hull. I watched David for the subtle change in speed and grace that would indicate he was Boosting. When I didn't see the changes, relief that he wasn't risking the damage Boost does to a body warred with consternation that he faced the mass of enemies without Boost's benefits.

"Hang on darling," I whispered. "Help is near!"

Then Thor's men reached David's position and he vanished into the swirling mass of hand-to-hand fighting.

LAST STAND ON THE VANGUARD

David

A barrage of blaster bolts blazed glowing trails in the dawn air, whizzing harmlessly past Captain Wright and me. Running and firing at such long range made accurate shots virtually impossible, especially for men with little training in their use. Within a few seconds, the rate of fire dropped off significantly before stopping all together.

A handful of our men returned fire with our captured blaster rifles. As with our foes, the rifles' power packs ran dry after only a few shots.

"Remember when I estimated those blaster rifles could fire twenty-five or more shots on a single charge?" I asked Wright. When he nodded, I said, "It appears I considerably overestimated."

"I am, of course, devastated to discover a member of the royal family is capable of a mistake of such magnitude, sir," Wright said.

"I'd be just a tad more likely to believe that if you weren't grinning quite so broadly, Captain."

With a horde of men three times our number charging down upon us, Wright threw back his head and laughed. As the men closest to us passed the explanation down the line, the laughter proved contagious. Nothing Wright or I said was all that funny, but pre-battle tension can amplify anything—worries become terrors and mildly amusing becomes hilarious. The thing about battle tension is that it affects both sides.

Fifty yards away, the men leading the charge saw Wright laugh as if he hadn't a care in the world. The tension worked on their minds, too. Seeing such relaxed behavior from an opponent surely gave them pause. Their steps faltered and their headlong charge slowed. The men behind the leading edge crashed into the slowing ones before them. Men tangled and fell, tripping up more men as they were trampled by their fellows.

The charge didn't break, but it sowed confusion among our enemies and, for a minute or so, reduced their number by almost a quarter. The men who reached the wreck of the *Vanguard* still yelled their battle cry, but some of the lust was gone from it.

Wright signaled his men and the rest of the *Vanguard's* crew gave voice to their own battle cry as they surged up from behind the airship's keel. Again, the leading edge of the charge faltered and our line crashed into them. Swords swung, blood flew, and the hollow hull thumped like a drum from the pounding of all the feet upon it.

Our line held for a few seconds before the fight broke into small pockets of swirling action. Wright and I formed a triangle with one of the airship's other officers, protecting each other's backs as we fought off the mass of attackers. Holding the high ground worked to our advantage, as any man we knocked backward was likely to tumble off the hull, taking one or two of his fellows down to the ground with him.

My sword rose and fell, swung and sliced, tore and thrust. Soon the bright silver blade Rob gave me was red with the blood of my enemies. My grip grew slick from sweat and a dull ache developed in my arm as it could never stop moving. With a clash of steel on steel, I deflected a thrust aimed at Wright's back. I reversed my swing, bringing the edge of the blade across the chest of the attacker. The man screamed and stumbled backward. I caught sight of two ribs exposed by my cut before the man tumbled out of my line of sight.

For a few precious seconds, the fight moved away from our trio. All three of us used those seconds to scan the battlefield. Knots of crewmen battled all around us and, to my biased eye, gave better than they got. But no matter how valiantly our men fought, the math still didn't work out for us. The crew had to take down three of Thor's men for every man we lost just to break even. Without easily defensible choke points, like we had inside the wreck, it was only a matter of time before we were overrun. Boosting might buy us a few extra minutes, but the end result would be the same.

As despair rose up from within, Wright caught my shoulder and pointed his sword to the west. "Sir, look over there!"

The *Tercel*, plainly visible in the dawn light, steamed our way at top speed!

NEW ALLIES
Callan

A young ensign brought a speaking trumpet to me as the *Tercel* closed on both Thor and the trogs. The young, eager face reminded me of Chris and I'm afraid my smile of thanks also bore a tinge of sadness. With a nod, the boy ran back to help with the preparations to capture Thor.

Under the supervision of the Marine Commander, lines were tied off along both sides of the airship. The plan involved Marines swinging down to the ground and subduing Thor while the *Tercel* drove on toward the wreck of the *Vanguard*. Any plan devised to speed help to David and his men while also capturing the rogue galactic had my full support.

When apprised of the plan, I'd given my approval and offered one suggestion. "If it's possible to pull Thor onboard without slowing down, please do so. He could be a handy tool for convincing his men to surrender. 'Without slowing down' is the vital phrase, Captain."

Jorson relayed that to the six men picked for the job. Within seconds, betting pools formed around the Marines' chances of dragging Thor back to the *Tercel* and which Marine might pull it off.

Meanwhile, fierce fighting ranged across the broken hull of the

Vanguard. Thor still had his back to us, yelling commands into a device I assumed was a comm. Were some of his men equipped with comms, as well, so Thor could direct the battle? I found myself hoping that was the case since Thor hadn't shown any indications of military training. His advantages lay in superior numbers and weaponry, though something must have happened to the blaster rifles. I'd watched a barrage of inaccurate shots at the beginning of the charge but nothing after that.

Tearing my eyes away from the battle, I moved to the railing as the airship approached the trogs. They'd stopped their jogging retreat at our approach, watching us with what must be wary eyes. Captain Jorson and I went to the airship's railing and gave a friendly wave to the trogs. The idea was to let them catch sight of Lady Death and to reassure them we offered no threat to them.

"Your Highness, could you hold off calling to the trogs until my Marines have swung down upon Thor?" Jorson asked. "The man's concentration is locked on the battle and I'd hate to draw his attention away from it."

"That's an excellent suggestion, Captain," I said.

As the ship passed by the trogs, their posture relaxed and they lowered their weapons. Curiosity kept them watching us, though, and several pointed when the Marines climbed atop the railing. I looked for Thor, but he was hidden by the *Tercel's* hull.

One after another, the Marines jumped from the railing and swung out of sight. I found myself holding my breath, waiting for the sound of blaster fire or the ring of steel. Before I heard either, a sudden cheer rose from the port railing and an officer yelled, "We've landed our catch, lads! Reel it in before it squirms off the hook."

"We've got him, Your Highness!" Jorson crowed.

Grinning, I turned back to the trogs. More of them pointed and though I couldn't hear their chuffing laughter, I saw many of them watching the scene with amusement. I raised the trumpet to my mouth and waved my other arm over my head.

"Trogs! I am Lady Death, the mate of the man you call the

Hand of Death. He fights against the coward you so recently served, the man who refused the Hand of Death's challenge for leadership, and the man we've just captured!" The trogs were falling behind quickly, so I skipped any other formalities and came to the point. "Come with us and join the Hand of Death in his fight. I give you my word you will be well rewarded if you do!"

I lowered the speaking trumpet and watched for any sign the trogs accepted my offer. Most of the trogs didn't understand Mordanian and required a translation from the few who did. Nothing happened for a few terribly long seconds, then a small group of trogs turned and ran after the *Tercel*. Another band followed, then two more, and then the whole mass of trogs was running in our wake!

I turned back to the deck in time to watch the crew hoist a Marine over the railing. He had one strong arm wrapped around Thor, managing to keep hold of him and pin his arms at the same time. Two more Marines took the galactic in hand while the one who captured him quickly and expertly removed every weapon and device Thor carried. The man presented them to me as the other two bound their sputtering, red-faced prisoner

"Well done, gentlemen," I cried. "Now let's go help the crew of the *Vanguard*!"

DEFEAT FROM THE JAWS OF VICTORY

David

My heart swelled with pride and renewed purpose at the sight of the mighty *Tercel* steaming our way. Even at this distance, we could make out Marines and airmen gathering along the railings and preparing to join the battle. If I could just be heard over the din of battle, maybe I could convince Thor's men to surrender and save lives on both sides. Captain Wright beat me to it.

"Vanguards!" Wright bellowed in a voice capable of carrying to all corners of an airship in combat. It easily rose over the clash of swords. "Our sister ship, the *Tercel*, comes from the west! Hold out for another minute and we'll have these blackguards outmanned and trapped between two forces!"

Silence descended as everyone turned and looked west. At the sight of the low-flying *Tercel*, our men roared in triumph. All around us, the will to fight leaked from our enemies. Their shoulders sagged, the blades dipped, and their eyes darted about as if frantically searching for some place to hide from the approaching airship.

The officer who fought with Wright and me took this quiet moment to note, "The trogs are charging along behind the *Tercel!*"

Hope flared in the faces of our enemies for a second, then Wright dashed it.

"The trogs must have switched to our side, Lieutenant Arnot. Otherwise, Captain Jorson would have his crossbowmen firing at them."

As Thor's men once again lost hope, I called, "Lay down your arms and surrender! On my honor, you'll be treated fairly."

A few men dropped their swords and it looked like we had the situation well in hand. Then four of Thor's men bolted, leaping from the *Vanguard's* hull and running off to the east. Then it was as if a dam broke and a hundred or more men ran off after them. Our men were too tired and too outnumbered to give pursuit.

"Let them go, men," Wright ordered. "We can round them up later."

"But sir," Arnot said, "Ensign Marlow led the girl, the other ensigns, and the ship's boys in that direction!"

Wright and I shielded our eyes as we looked directly into the rising sun. Not more than two hundred yards ahead of the mass of retreating men ran a band of small figures. They stumbled and staggered, obviously exhausted from the overwork in Thor's base and a sleepless night filled with running and fighting. Excited shouts rose from some of Thor's men as they caught sight of the group ahead of them.

"They'll take the lass and those lads hostage and bargain the children's lives against their own freedom," Wright said. He looked back over his shoulder at the *Tercel*. "Captain Jorson won't know to pursue until he gets here and I doubt he could reach the youngsters in time, anyway."

My mind went back six years to our return to Aashla after defeating the space pirates and establishing contact with the Terran Federation. I felt again the horrible anguish as Callan and I told Kim that Milo, her younger brother and the last of her family, died so I could live. I saw again the wracking grief that overcame Kim as we delivered the news.

I knew Chris and Jade well enough to feel certain they would put up a fight against Thor's men. I knew Mordanian ensigns well enough to know they'd follow Chris's lead. And I knew Thor's followers well enough to know they would probably kill several of the children while trying to subdue them.

These thoughts must have shown on my face because Captain Wright said, "I don't think there's anything we can do to help them, sir."

"Like hell," I said and jumped to the ground.

Boost!

As soon as my implant received the command, it flooded my body with adrenaline and my fatigue vanished. I was running as soon as I hit the ground, tearing across the desert in long, strong, inhumanly fast strides. I was dimly aware of the cheering voices of the *Vanguard's* crew before I tuned out everything except the backs of the men running ahead of me. The ground blurred beneath my feet as I rapidly closed in on the trailing edge of the retreating men. I considered simply hacking my way through them in the hopes of drawing all attention to me and away from the fleeing children. Certain that would make the leaders all the more desperate to reach Chris and the others, I tried another tack.

"Clear the way or die!" I shouted when I was no more than ten yards from the closest men.

Several looked over their shoulders to see who shouted. Their eyes widened when they saw me bearing down on them. With my churning legs and raised sword, I hoped I was the embodiment of my trog nickname.

Never one to pass up a chance to spout lines like you'd hear in an adventure vid, I added, "Give way before the Hand of Death or feel his wrath!"

To my relief, the men dove aside and I charged into the middle of the mass of men. I gave voice to a wordless battle cry and more men turned to see what was approaching. Some cleared the way, some froze in shock, and others ran all the harder to get away from me. I dodged around one man before swinging my sword in a wide arc before me. The blade sliced across the backs of three men. They all screamed in pain and stumbled.

I leapt at the man directly ahead of me, pushing him farther down before planting a foot on his shoulder and springing forward. I passed over a couple of men who watched me with goggle-eyed astonishment. I saw no open ground to land on so, using the quickness Boost gave me, landed on another shoulder. I felt bone crack beneath my boot as I ran on. I used another man's head for my next step, driving the man to his knees as I sprang away.

This time, I came down on open ground with only two men between me and the kids. Those men spun to face me, swords swinging in unison. I beat aside the attack from my right and simply caught the other man's sword arm with my free hand. In riposte, I drove my sword through the man on the right. At the same time, I twisted the other man's arm and yanked down. His wrist broke and his shoulder popped out of its socket. Yanking my sword free, I ran past the dying man and into the open.

Fifteen yards ahead of me, Chris, Jade, and the rest of the youngsters stood with weapons ready. Jade and one of the ship's boys held blaster rifles and the others held blades. Their chests heaved from the run and their arms shook with fatigue, but they all wore looks of grim determination that gave way to wonder as I burst from the mob of men.

The charging men ground to a halt, still trying to figure out what had happened. I stopped in the open ground between the two groups and spun to face the men.

"You'll have to go through me to get to these children," I said, struggling against Boost to speak slowly and clearly. "The first man who makes a move toward them will die on the end of my blade. As will the second. And the third. And however many others I have to kill before the *Tercel* arrives."

A voice called from inside the mob, "He can't kill us all! Get him!"

The men before me surged forward.

A FINAL SACRIFICE

Callan

Much as I wanted to watch the battle and reassure myself David was safe, I knew Thor could be the key to ending the conflict as soon as possible. Turning back to him, I studied the devices the Marine took from Thor. I couldn't figure out what most of the things did, but two were obvious. Keeping the blaster pistol and the comm, I handed all but those two items back to the Marine who captured him, then ordered the Marines holding Thor to bring him to the bow rail.

"Your men are going to lose, Thor," I said, pointing at the distant battle. "This is your chance to save a few lives. When I hold the comm to your mouth, order your men to surrender."

Thor laughed, drawing a rough shake and glares from the Marines. One of them said, "Show some respect!"

"Or what? You'll kill me?" Thor looked me in the eyes, calm despite the situation. "I could not care less about the lives of any of those men fighting over there. If their deaths can also buy the death of your planet-despoiling husband, I'll die knowing my sacrifice was worthwhile."

I cursed myself silently for not turning the comm on before speaking to this strange man. That one admission could have spurred exactly the surrender I wanted. I thumbed the unit on, hoping Thor might see fit to say something equally damning.

"I don't understand you one bit," I said. "How can you hate humanity so much that you're willing to throw away the lives of those who serve you?"

Shifting his eyes to the comm, Thor smiled and said, "The Mordanians have taken me. Press the attack and avenge me!"

I nodded at one of the Marines and a fist slammed into Thor's stomach. His breath whooshed out of him, leaving him incapable of speaking. Raising the comm, I said, "This is Her Royal Highness Princess Callan of Mordan. Throw down your arms and surrender. You have my word you'll receive fair treatment and fair trials."

"Well, well, if it isn't the media darling herself," said an unknown, feminine voice. "I've turned off the links to the comms worn by our men. They haven't heard a word since you first turned the comm on."

"And you must be the lady of the base. Freya, isn't it?" I replied.

"That's the name I've used on this operation."

"I don't suppose you'd be willing to tell me your real name?" I asked. "I so dislike using false names."

"Says the woman who uses one name and three titles when introducing herself," Freya sneered. "Besides, I haven't used my birth name in decades. You'll just have to make do with what you know."

"Have it your way. I'm sure the Terran Federation will discover your real name when we turn you over to them."

Soft and sultry laughter came from the comm. "You're not going to capture me, little princess, and you're not going to hold Thor for much longer."

Despite his wheezing, Thor managed to gasp out, "Farewell, my love. Savor this revenge!"

I looked at the man in alarm, recognizing someone accepting the idea of his own death. "Throw him overboard!"

The Marines didn't hesitate, tossing Thor over the railing immediately. The Marine who had captured him tackled me to the deck a second before the explosion. With sickening splats, pieces of Thor landed on the deck. A thin red mist rose next to the *Tercel* before drifting away on the wind.

"Are you hurt, Your Highness?" demanded the Marine who tackled me.

All around us, officers and airmen rushed to our aid. Men shouted as I tried to reassure everyone. Then Dr. Mach pushed through the crowd and knelt next to me.

The doctor's eyes roamed over my body with a detached professionalism I rarely received from men. "I don't see any injuries, Your Highness. How do you feel?"

"I feel quite grateful to the Sergeant and his men for their quick reactions, Doctor. Now, if you would all stop hovering, I'd like to get up." I smiled to take any possible sting from my words. Once back on my feet, I turned to Captain Jorson and asked, "How goes the battle?"

Now reassured I was unhurt, the crew quickly turned their attention back to the battle. Seconds later, Jorson said, "The *Tercel* has been seen, Your Highness, and it looks like our arrival has taken the fight out of our enemies. They're surrendering."

A cheer rose from the crew and I felt my knot of tension loosen. Lieutenant Tucker, his spyglass still raised to his eye, spoke over the cheers, "A good hundred of the cowards have taken to their heels, Captain, and are running off into the desert."

Grinning broadly, Captain Jorson said, "A fat lot of good that will do for them, eh? They'll come crawling back to surrender when they get thirsty!"

"I am less certain of that, sir," Tucker replied as he unconsciously leaned forward. "It looks like Captain Rice has Boosted and is pursuing them!"

My knot of tension tightened once again. "Can you see why he's chasing them, Lieutenant?"

"I'm looking, Your Highness, but—" Tucker froze for an interminable second, his glass locked on something far beyond my unaided sight. "Good God, it's the *Vanguard's* ensigns, the ship's boys, and a young woman! An officer must have ordered them away before the battle began, but they're too tired to run fast. If Thor's men catch them, they'll negotiate the lives of the youngsters against their own freedom!"

"Does the crew of the *Vanguard* have their situation well in hand?" I asked.

Jorson swung his spyglass back to the wrecked airship. "They do, Your Highness. Shall we go to Captain Rice's aid?"

"Yes, Captain, and at all possible speed," I replied, silently praying we could reach David in time.

"Mister Carson!" Jorson called across the deck. "We need all the speed you can coax from the engines!"

"Aye aye, sir!" Carson said, unabashed glee evident in his voice. "And thank you, sir!"

The roar of the engines increased immediately. The airship's big propellers thrummed louder as they spun faster and faster. To my surprise, I had to catch hold of the railing to keep from losing my balance as the big airship surged forward. The *Vanguard's* crew waved as we passed overhead, cheering us onward.

I raised a hand to shield my eyes as I squinted into the bright morning sunlight. I made out a single figure—David, of course—standing between the mob of men and the children. Then, to my horror, the men sprang toward my husband!

HOLD THE LINE

David

I ncited by someone who wasn't on the front line, the men before me raised their swords and charged. With Boost-supplied adrenaline still burning through my veins, I leapt forward with quickness impossible for normal men. My sword flashed in the morning light as I swung it at the nearest attacker. The man's battle cry turned to a gurgle as my razor-sharp blade sliced through his throat. Hot blood sprayed into the air, adding more red stains to my already-ruined clothes. I carried the stroke past the dying man and cut the arm of the man next to him down to the bone. He stumbled aside, screaming, as I danced back out of range of the slow counter-attacks aimed at me.

My feet shuffled through the sand and rocks, giving me another idea. Digging a foot into the loose ground, I kicked up at the mob in front of me. Sand, dust, and rocks pelted the men before me and several of them clapped hands to their eyes. I lunged at one, driving a foot of bloody blade into his gut. Twisting the blade, I pulled it free. I saw the man's eyes go wide in shock before the fight drew my attention elsewhere.

Skipping backward again, I parried two attacks but was unable to find the time to return the attack. From the corner of my eye, I saw the bright glint of steel on my right side and one of my attackers fell as a sword stabbed completely through his thigh. Another flash came from my left and the other attacker barely managed to parry a thrust aimed at his heart. Then the crack of blaster rifles opened up behind us and men on both of our far flanks fell before the shooting of Jade and the ship's boy.

"Sorry we're late, sir," Chris said from my right. "We had a tad more ground to cover than you did."

A quick glance to either side showed Chris and the other three ensigns from the *Vanguard* standing beside me. All four wore the set expressions of frightened young men determined to master their fear and do their duty.

"It's good to have you men by my side," I said, hoping my calm appreciation of their aid might settle their nerves a bit. "All we have to do is hold our line until the *Tercel* arrives."

I shuffled forward on the loose terrain and feinted a low thrust against the man before me. As soon as his sword dipped, I reversed direction and sliced upward. Instinctively, the man pulled his hips back to protect his groin and presented his chest to my blade. It sliced through clothing and skin, opening a deep gash from his stomach to his breastbone.

As I stepped back into line with the ensigns, another round of blaster bolts burned the men trying to work their way around our line. I said, "Don't worry overmuch about the flanks, men. It seems our companions have that well in hand."

The mob spread out before us and the men on the far ends edged their way forward in an attempt to fully encircle us all.

To either side of me, the young men held their line, showing just how effective a little discipline and teamwork can be against a mob. But that advantage would vanish as soon as our enemies flanked us.

"Fall back toward Jade and the ship's boys, lads," I ordered. "Take it steady and maintain discipline."

Blades clashed and flashed and it seemed I was the only one able to score an effective hit. Then the Ensign on the far left gave a cry and stumbled backward. His sword fell from fingers that refused to obey his commands and his free hand clapped over a deep cut in his shoulder. The man who cut him raised a fist and yelled in triumph—then a blaster bolt struck him in the forehead and he slowly toppled backward.

Behind me, Jade muttered, "Take that, you son of a—"

Jade's next word was drowned out by screams from both sides of us. Looking to my left, I saw a massive ballista bolt impaling four men. More men lay bleeding and screaming along the bolt's path. A quick glance to the right showed a similar scene. Then men before me cried out and pitched to the ground, crossbow quarrels sticking out of them.

Over the screams, I clearly heard Captain Jorson bellow, "Marines, away! Crossbowmen, reload and fire at will!"

The *Tercel* was here!

With a full-throated roar, the airship's Marine contingent swung down to attack. Each of them released their rope on the upswing. They flew at our enemies' rear line, swords raised and teeth bared. Landing just outside of sword-thrust range, the Marines waded into the poorly trained men with obvious relish. Then another hail of crossbow quarrels rained down on the remnants of Thor's army and more men cried and fell.

Jorson's voice cut through the din of battle easily. "Any man who drops his sword and goes to his knees will not be harmed!"

Almost as one, the men before us released their weapons and dropped to the ground. Two men didn't get the message and the Marines cut them down. And then the fight was over.

Dropping Boost, I rushed to the wounded Ensign and eased him down to the ground. He struggled gamely not to cry, but tears shone in his eyes.

"Captain, we need a doctor!" I called.

"He's on his way, sir," Jorson responded.

"Are you hurt, David?" Callan's lilting voice carried over the after-battle noise as Jorson's did.

"I'm fine, dear, thanks to Chris and the other ensigns."

"*Chris?*" Callan cried in wonder. "He's alive?"

"I am Your Highness," Chris responded. "Please forgive me if my actions caused you any distress!"

Then Dr. Mach bustled up and bent over the wounded Ensign. Cutting away the young man's shirt, Mach said jovially, "Ah, that's going to leave quite the lovely scar, Ensign Parnel. The young ladies are going to be *very* impressed!"

Looking up, Mach quietly added, "I need to close that wound now. I'm afraid I'm going to need a couple of men to hold the lad still."

Chris dropped to his knees next to his fellow Ensign. "Just tell me what to do, sir."

Perhaps remembering the somewhat queasy young Ensign he'd seen at the start of it all, Mach eyed Chris critically. "Are you sure you're up to it, Ensign?"

Chris returned the doctor's gaze calmly. "Of course, sir."

Mach gave a quick nod. "Yes, I believe you are."

Minutes later, with the Ensign's wound tightly stitched, the doctor oversaw lifting the wounded young man up to the *Tercel*. Chris and I rose to feet and found ourselves confronted by the only two women present. Callan ran her eyes over me, no doubt assuring herself I really was unhurt. Jade skipped that step and grabbed Chris in a fierce hug.

As my wife wrapped her arms around me, she watched the teenagers with a smile. "I think they make a lovely couple, don't you, darling?"

I nodded. "And they managed to find each other without any help from you or your mother."

Just as I bent close to kiss Callan, there was a flash of light from the mountain behind us. Its ground shook and, seconds later, we heard the sound of a massive explosion!

TREACHEROUS FREYA

Callan

David and I whirled to face the mountain a few miles off. Dust billowed all about Thor's base, blocking our view. The wind slowly carried the dust away, revealing the mountaintop in time for us to see some of the surface crumble and collapse in on itself.

"It looks like someone collapsed the cave entrance we discovered..." David's voice trailed off for a moment. "God, can it only have been yesterday morning?"

I took out the comm the Marine had taken from Thor and stared at it. "Was any of this really worth dying for, Freya?"

David cocked his head, eying the comm. "Where did-"

I realized I hadn't turned off the comm when Freya's voice issued from it. "You're right, little princess, none of this was worth my life. It *was* worth a lot of other people's lives, though. In that light, I'm sure you can understand why I wasn't in that ridiculous mountain base."

I stared at the comm unit with incredulity. "No, Freya, I can't understand any of this."

David gently took the comm from me and spoke into it. "This whole situation is extremely convoluted and expensive—especially for an AFIP operation. You guys are usually quite straightforward

—find a way to arm the primitives and then attack the nearest human city. I didn't even know AFIP had the skill and resources to do something as delicate as implant surgery."

Freya laughed merrily, "Yes, the fippers are a depressingly direct bunch of idiots. And no, left to themselves they couldn't have stolen working diplomatic and military implants, much less surgically installed them. They were quite happy to have a 'recruit' who could do both. Thor was happy to finally have a lover who shared his beliefs. And that exiled princeling was quite excited to get his implant. Men are *so* easy to manipulate—dangle power, sex, or revenge before them and they'll fall all over themselves to do your bidding. I'm sure the little princess knows exactly what I mean. I've seen how you fawn over her, Rice."

Confusion spread over David's face. "You're not a fipper?"

"My, you are slow on the uptake. And here I thought you Scouts were supposed to be smart. Maybe all that honor, oath, duty, and trustworthiness dulls the mind," Freya said, her voice thick with condescension. "Why don't you be a good little man and hand the comm back to the princess."

I took the comm back from David. "I don't know who you think you are, you pathetic woman, but you do not threaten *my* planet, kill *my* people, and insult *my* husband! You sound just like one of those supercilious galactic diplomats I've dealt with ever since Aashla established contact with the Terran Federation. You expect us to fall all over ourselves to get our hands on your cast off technological baubles and then act surprised and offended when we don't sign over all of our mineral rights for a pile of cheap crap. You and your kind make me sick."

"A very impassioned speech, little princess. No wonder everyone either loves or loathes you," Freya replied. "Anyway, it's been fun chatting but now it's time for me to get on with my real mission."

"You do realize you're going to stand out here on Aashla," I said. "You don't know our customs and you sure the hell don't understand a woman's position in this world."

"You'd be amazed how much information the Federation has gathered on your world, little princess," Freya sneered, "and it's all stored in my implant. So don't you worry about me—I'll fit right in."

I laughed at Freya and it was not a pleasant sound. "Thank you, Freya. We'd have caught you eventually, but now I know we'll have you within a day or two."

"Nice try, princess, but I know better," Freya said. "I might die from bad luck—barbaric worlds like yours have all sorts of ways to kill—but no one will capture me. I'm just that good at what I do."

"I'm sure you'll believe that right up until you find yourself standing before me in the Mordanian Court," I said. "Then I'll teach you the true meaning of *barbaric*. You will beg me for the blessed release of death before I'm finished with you."

I thumbed the comm unit off and dropped it in a pocket. Looking up, I found David, Jade, and Chris staring at me.

"What?" I asked.

A leer spread across David's face. "God, you're sexy when you play the barbaric princess!"

Chris and Jade blushed bright crimson and quickly turned away.

"I wasn't playing, David—at least not entirely. That woman has a lot to pay for and I am going to collect her debt." I said. Running a finger lazily down David's arm, I flashed my best sultry smile and added, "But I'll be happy to treat you to a night of enthusiastic barbarism when we get home."

"But how are you going to capture one woman out of millions?" David asked. "That's hard enough on a Federation world where everyone carries identification and every transaction leaves a digital footprint. But here-"

"Even though you've lived here for nine years, David, sometimes you still think like a Federation citizen," I said. "Freya admitted she has an implant and the Federation has sensors capable of finding anyone with one."

"Sure they can, but the implants don't broadcast the owner's identity," David said. "Do you have any idea how many people have implants?"

"On your home world, millions," I said. "On Aashla, eighty-six. Eighty-seven if you count Freya."

David's eyes widened in surprise. "You're right, I was still thinking like a Federation citizen."

"And so is Freya," I said. "I'd love to see the look on her face when she's captured."

From the deck of the *Tercel*, we heard Captain Jorson issuing orders and organizing teams to return to the mountain base and search for survivors. David looked up at the airship and said, "I should join one of those teams."

"You most certainly should not, darling! How many times have you Boosted since you last slept?" I asked. When David looked down sheepishly without answering, I continued, "That's what I thought. You're going to rest and get something to eat. The Mordanian Navy will find a way to manage without your help."

A few feet away, Jade said, "David hasn't removed you from my care, Chris, and it's my opinion you are too injured to join a search team."

"But Jade-" Chris tried to protest.

"Don't make me appeal to a higher power, Ensign!" Jade said. "I am certain Callan—um, Her Highness—will agree with me."

"She's right, Chris," I said to the teenagers. "But since you desperately want to do something useful, you can take one of the *Tercel's* pinnaces and escort Jade back to her family."

Jade looked distinctly uncomfortable at my suggestion. "Dad's going to be awfully mad at me for flying off."

"But he'll be even more relieved to know you're safe," I said. "Chris, are you up to this onerous duty?"

"Flying a pinnace?" Chris asked. "Sure."

I shook my head. "I meant are you up to meeting Jade's parents? For some reason young men always get nervous about that."

"Um, I think so?" Chris replied.

"Just let Jade introduce you, Chris," David said. "You risked your own life to save hers. Fathers tend to appreciate that sort of thing."

"It sounds like I've missed all sorts of excitement," I said, linking my arm in David's. "Let's board the *Tercel* and you can tell me all about it while the crew prepares a pinnace."

David let Jade and Chris tell most of the story, only speaking up to downplay his own role or to highlight the courage of others. By the time Jade and Chris left in the pinnace—Jade pulled rank on Chris and took the controls—I had most of the story. David was asleep before the pinnace was out of sight.

BACK TO MY PARENTS

Jade

Chris sat quietly across from me as I piloted the pinnace away from the *Tercel*. Within minutes, our surroundings were as quiet as Chris. After all of the noise and activity of the last twelve hours, the clank and hiss of the pinnace's steam engine barely registered in my ears. It obviously didn't bother Chris, as his head slowly sank toward his chest. He caught himself and jerked his head up, embarrassment evident on his face.

"You look worn out, Chris," I said. "When did you sleep last?"

Chris turned bleary eyes toward me. "Um... Two nights ago? No, three. I think."

"Why don't you take a nap?"

Chris straightened his back and shoulders briefly. They began settling in weariness before he started speaking. "This is a Naval vessel. As the only officer onboard, it's my duty to maintain watch."

I rolled my eyes. Why were boys so stubborn? "David made me part of the Royal Navy *and* put you under my orders. That lasts until I'm returned to my family."

"We're on our way to do that now," Chris said.

"But we haven't done it yet." Chris didn't look convinced, so I tried the best metaphor I could think of. "Is 'transporting cargo' the same as 'delivering cargo'?"

"No." Chris smiled in resignation. "Very well, Captain Jade, I am yours to command. What do you wish me to do?"

Adopting the annoying tone of voice Mrs. Sune always used with me, I said, "Sit next to me, Ensign Chris."

"Aye aye!" He grinned and joined me on the port side of the pinnace.

"Now, kiss me." I felt my cheeks heat up at my own temerity.

Chris must have seen my blush, because he gave me a simple peck on a red cheek. "As you command, Captain Jade."

"That's a fine kiss, Ensign—if I was your sister!" I glared at Chris. "Kiss me like you mean it. Kiss me like...like..."

As I floundered for the right word, Chris blushed deeply. "Like a...lover?"

As Chris leaned into me, I breathed, "Yes."

It was more than one kiss and they were all really, truly wonderful. Finally, Chris's exhaustion got the better of him. He leaned back, his eyes barely open, and began scooting down the bench seat. I caught his arm.

"Lay your head in my lap, Chris. You'll be more comfortable."

Even as his head sank down, he murmured, "But what about you?"

I stroked his hair and whispered, "I'll be more comfortable, too."

By the time the wreck of the *Wind Dancer* came into view, Chris had his face pressed up against my stomach with his arms wrapped around me. And I hadn't been so comfortable since I was a little girl sitting in my father's lap.

My parents and a crowd of crewmen gathered as I arrived. The men took lines from the pinnace and held them in place while I began venting gas.

"I'd like a few choice words with you, young lady," Dad all but bellowed.

I put a finger to my lips and looked down at the head cradled in my lap. "Shhh! Chris—ah, Ensign Marlow is sleeping."

"Who—and far more importantly, *where*—is this Ensign, Jade?" If anything, Dad's voice was even louder.

Once again, I felt my cheeks color. God in heaven, I felt like I'd blushed more in this one day than I had in my entire life!.

Dad reacted like a typical father and began knocking on the pinnace's hull. "Wake up, Ensign Marlow! If your head is where I think it is, you've got some explaining to do!"

"Mom!" I turned an imploring look toward her, hoping she'd restrain Dad.

With a nod in my direction, Mom caught hold of Dad's arm. "Now, Lon, you're overreacting."

"Overreacting?" Dad's voice was just as loud, but at least he wasn't knocking on the hull any more. "Some Navy boy has his head in my little girl's lap and you say I'm overreacting?"

"Dear, Jade is sixteen. She's hardly a little girl anymore." Dad opened his mouth to argue, but Mom put a finger over his mouth. "Do I need to remind you that I was Jade's age when you convinced me to go skinny dipping in the river?"

"*What?*" My eyes went wide at the thought of my parents getting naked together a couple of years before they got married.

All of Dad's yelling and knocking didn't wake Chris up. My reaction to Mom's announcement did the trick, though.

Chris sat up slowly, his eyes barely open. In a drowsy voice, he asked, "What are we talking about?"

My mind still reeling, I said, "Skinny dipping."

"Oh. That sounds like fun." Then his head dropped back into my lap. It stayed there for a split second, then his eyes flew wide. Chris sat bolt upright and looked at Dad in panic. "I'm sorry, sir! I didn't know what I was saying."

"Yes," Dad drawled. "Jade does have that effect on people."

Chris jumped to his feet and saluted. "Ensign Christopher Marlow returning your daughter to you, sir!"

"Duly noted, Ensign Marlow," Dad responded, waving Chris to stand at ease. "I suppose you'll be returning to your airship now?"

Mom gave Chris a maternal look. "The boy is absolutely worn out, Lon. He's not in any shape to pilot the pinnace right now."

Dad's tone sharpened again. "Ensign, can I assume none of that exhaustion has anything to do with my daughter?"

Too tired to see the potential trap, Chris said, "Not all of it, sir."

That set Dad off again. "And just *what* have you been doing with Jade?"

This time, I spoke before Chris could. "He's been saving my life, Dad. And risking his own to do it!"

Dad looked my way. "Eh? Are you serious, Jade?"

"Yes, Dad. David will confirm it next time you see him." Without waiting to be asked, I told the short version of how Chris saved me from plunging to my death.

By the time I finished, the pinnace was low enough for us to debark. Dad helped Chris down and offered his hand to the Ensign. "Please forgive a father his suspicions, Ensign."

"You just want to protect Jade, sir." Chris turned a smile my way. "I feel the same way about her."

Before their conversation could get any more embarrassing, Mom swooped in with a hug for Chris and then one for me. She made sure we got something to eat, listened to my account of everything that happened after I sailed off in the pinnace, and then laid some blankets out in the shade of large section of the *Wind Dancer's* wreckage. She didn't even bat an eye when I insisted on sleeping next to Chris.

Mom kissed him lightly on the cheek. "Thank you for saving my daughter, Chris."

His breathing deepened even before Mom turned her attention to me. She ran a hand through my hair. "He strikes me as a fine young man, Jade. I think he'll dedicate his life to you, if you give him the chance."

I loved hearing her say that, but I still felt a perverse need to disagree. "I haven't even known him for an entire day, Mom!"

"And yet the two of you have been through more in that time than many couples go through in a lifetime."

I ducked my head, too embarrassed to look at Mom. "Do you believe in love at first sight?"

"I most certainly do, Jade." She kissed me on the forehead. "And you're living proof of it."

"I knew Chris was the boy for me the second he swung into the cliff and wrapped his arm around me." I snuggled up against Chris. My eyes were growing heavy, but I felt compelled to ask her one question. "Did you really go skinny dipping with Dad when you were sixteen?"

Mom nodded. "Your father was a silver-tongued devil—still is. He tried to talk me into more, but I made him marry me before he got that."

Drowsiness made me more daring. "Does that mean you won't mind if I want to go skinny dipping with Chris sometime?"

Mom actually laughed. Standing, she said, "Why don't we worry about that when there's some water to dip your skin in?"

Then my eyes closed and, arms wrapped around Chris, I joined him in sleep.

AFTERMATH

David

The search crews pulled twenty-three survivors and eighteen bodies from the remains of Thor's base. Among the survivors was Jade's former sort-of-boyfriend Forbose. From interviews with the survivors, it's estimated as many as sixty bodies still lay buried under the mountain. The survivors were placed under guard, each of them destined for a trial sometime in the future.

Forbose was the most popular of the prisoners, though I believe the boy would have happily passed on that honor. Alas, I couldn't be there when Jade visited him. According to Jade's mother, the slap Jade gave the boy is probably still echoing through the mountains.

I suspect Forbose preferred the slap to his confrontation with Jade's father, which boiled down to the warning, "If you come near my little girl again you'll *wish* you were dead and buried under that mountain."

Chris and the two *Vanguard* crewmen Forbose was abusing when Chris punched the larger boy also paid a visit to Forbose. They never touched him, but Jade told me Forbose was white as a sheet when the trio left.

It took the Federation less than a day to locate Freya traveling toward the southern city-states. A consulate aircar delivered her to Mordanian authorities a few hours later. Freya wore an expression of utter disbelief when she was dragged into the Mordanian Court a few days later. Callan took quite a bit of pleasure in Freya's reaction.

Freya refused to cooperate with the Federation and she proved capable of defeating their best interrogation drugs. Callan, as promised, put her civilized behavior aside and brought forth the barbarian princess. She doesn't like doing that but, after spending the day attending funerals for the airmen killed in storm-induced crashes and in the battle against Thor's army, she readily gave the orders. Freya turned out to be a typical galactic citizen in one respect—she never believed she would face anything more than a prison sentence for her crimes. She remained in denial right up until she was taken into an interrogation room and strapped to a table. Freya broke when the interrogator carefully explained the purpose for each of his blades.

She works for a shadowy organization loosely associated with some of the Terran Federation's neighbors—most particularly the Waaglar Combine and the Star Empire of Cromia. Somehow, her organization had smuggled a sensor drone into the system. Based on the drone's findings, the Aashlan system has anywhere from three to five wormholes besides the one we all knew about. Wormholes represent huge opportunities for economic expansion, so Freya's mission was broadened. While the other governments hoped Aashla might join them, their primary goal was keeping us out of the Federation. The false fipper operation was designed to throw the Federation into a poor light and give the other governments the chance to forge alliances with us. In the end, it did the exact opposite, pushing several previously neutral countries toward favoring Federation membership.

Freya's trial was short and the outcome was never in doubt. She's now a guest at the Mordanian Women's Prison awaiting a date with the headsman. Word is that Freya believes the sentence is just for show and will never be carried out. All I can say is the woman is in for a very big, though very brief, surprise.

HOME AT LAST

Chris

By the time we headed home, half-a-dozen Mordanian Naval ships were on hand. I was given a place on the *Tercel* and assigned to light duty because of my injuries. I'd much rather have sailed on the *Peregrine*, where Jade and her family were berthed, but Captain Jorson insisted the surviving Vanguards travel with him. It was meant as a show of respect and I was honored by the Captain's gesture. I just wished I had Jade at my side.

Callan and David were also aboard and they paid special attention to me, regularly inviting me to dine with them and the ship's officers. Her Highness even gave me a pair of Terran made binoculars so I could more clearly see Jade standing on the deck of the *Peregrine* and gazing my way.

It took four days to reach Morda. When we docked, I had one important duty before I could find Jade. The surviving crew of the *Vanguard* and the *Tercel* formed an honor guard for our fallen comrades. We escorted the coffins—constructed from the *Vanguard's* wreckage—from the dock to the Naval Cemetery. A special burial service is planned in two days. Until then, the crews were given leave. Though we were all free to go, the surviving Vanguards lingered at the cemetery for a while, offering comfort to the families of the men who died. It was mid-afternoon by the time I left.

My family had been present to greet me when we docked, but returned home after paying their respects to the dead. I knew they were expecting me to come straight home, but I went looking for Jade, instead. Fortunately, Captain Wright offered his assistance. Officials who would have turned a deaf ear to a mere ensign readily offered information to a captain—particularly the captain of the *Vanguard*. Sooner than I had dared hope, I stood in the public room of the city's finest inn while a servant took a message to the Cochrans.

A few minutes later, my heart leapt when Jade descended the stairs. Then my heart leapt into my throat when I saw her parents descending right behind her. After four days apart, I'd hoped for a less restrained reunion. Jade's parents—intentionally or not—put a damper on that plan. I bowed to Mr. and Mrs. Cochran and gave Jade's hand a chaste kiss. Jade was equally reserved, though her eyes promised a lover's kiss when we were alone.

"Hello, Christopher," Mrs. Cochran said, giving me a maternal hug. "Are your injuries healing well?"

"Quite well, ma'am," I replied.

"I'm happy to hear that," she said.

Mr. Cochran went right to the point. "Your message requested permission to take Jade out for the evening. Where would you like to take her?"

"To meet my family, sir," I replied, "and join us for dinner."

Mr. Cochran looked at Jade and cocked an eyebrow. "And would you like to meet Chris's family, young lady?"

Jade didn't even flinch at the thought. "Yes."

"Nell, what do you think?"

"Oh, stop being so formal, Lon," Mrs. Cochran said. "Of course, Jade can go with Chris. Just have her back here by ten o'clock."

"How about eleven, Mom?" Jade asked.

"How about ten-thirty?" Mrs. Cochran compromised.

We agreed on the time and the Cochrans watched me walk away with their daughter. I offered her my arm, which she accepted, and we behaved ourselves all the way down the street and around a corner. Then Jade pulled me into the first alley and kissed me quite thoroughly. After the kiss, we just held each other for a while.

"I missed you so much, Chris," Jade breathed in my ear.

"I missed you, as well," I said, and returned her kiss with one of my own.

We spent quite a few minutes catching up like that, drawing curious glances from passersby. Most of them were amused. A few were scandalized, including one elderly woman who took it upon herself to instruct us on proper etiquette.

"You should stop this disgraceful public display at once!" Her mouth turned down in supreme disapproval as she waved a finger under Jade's nose. "Young lady, what are you saving for marriage?"

"I'm saving what comes after the kissing." Jade grinned at the woman's shocked reaction.

I steered Jade around the woman, tipping my hat at her frown. "It's time we were leaving anyway."

Soon enough, we reached my old neighborhood and word spread quickly that I was back. Tony saw me first and rushed over to greet me. His eyes widened when he realized I was holding hands with the girl standing next to me. Then a big grin lit up his face.

"There has *got* to be a great story behind this development," he said.

"I'm happy to see you again, too," I said.

"Yeah, welcome back blah blah blah." Tony turned to Jade and his grin widened. "Leave it to the smartest kid in the neighborhood to go off on a boring cruise and—if the news stories are right —play a major part in the biggest story in ages. *And* he came back with a pretty girl in tow!"

I turned to Jade. "The guy with no manners is my long-time friend, Tony Collins. Tony, meet Jade Cochran."

Jade released my hand to give Tony a proper handshake. That's when Becca came flying out of her house, running straight for me. Her face was flushed and her eyes glowed with excitement.

"Chris, you're back!" she cried, her tone one she'd never used with me in all of our seventeen years as neighbors. "I've been waiting for you!"

I realized she wasn't going to stop, so braced myself and held my arms out to catch her. Becca's arms were wide to embrace me, so I really wasn't sure how I was going to stop her without getting way too familiar with her. Fortunately, Tony caught Becca around the waist and stopped her.

"You let go of me right now, Anthony Collins," Becca commanded. "I need to give our new hero a proper welcome."

Aware that Jade was watching all of this with a bemused expression, I said, "I thought Sam was the big hero."

"Humph," Becca replied, struggling to get free of Tony's hold. "Did you know he made up that whole story about fighting raiders?"

"Yes, I did. Anyone who knows anything about airships and actual fighting would have known." I turned to Jade. "You'd have loved the story. It was full of crisp, turn-on-a-penny maneuvers performed by a heavily laden merchant ship and raider battles that ranged all over the deck and up into the rigging."

Becca, noticing Jade for the first time, stopped struggling and looked Jade up and down. "And just *who* is this, Chris?"

I wrapped an arm around Jade, pulling her close. "Becca, this is Jade Cochran, my companion in adventure and the love of my life."

Jade's expression cleared at my pronouncement. She smiled at Becca. "Pleased to meet you, Becca."

Becca's mouth opened and closed several times before she finally found her voice. "Don't be silly, Chris. *I'm* the love of your life!"

I shook my head sadly. "No, Becca, you're a silly girl who falls in love with stories, not people. Now, if you'll excuse us, my family is waiting for me."

Jade and I walked around a stunned Becca. Tony gave me a little wave and then placed a comforting hand on Becca's shoulder. He grinned broadly when she laid her head on his shoulder and cried.

"She's very pretty," Jade said. "Were you in love with her?"

"I thought I was, but now I know that was just an infatuation with the prettiest girl in the neighborhood."

I opened the door to my family home and the familiar noise of Marlow family life blared at us. The usual chaos kept anyone from noticing us until I conspicuously slammed the front door. Carrie, the youngest except for me, noticed us before anyone else.

Every Marlow has a voice that cuts through the usual commotion, but Carrie's is particularly piercing. "Chris is home—and he brought a *girl!*"

And then it was all hugs for me and introductions and hugs for Jade and stories and food. Lots and lots of food. In other words, it was home.

ROYAL RECOGNITION

David

T he day after Freya's trial, the crew of the *Tercel* lined up behind the surviving crew from the *Vanguard* in the palace's largest audience chamber. King Edwar and Queen Elaina officially presided over the ceremony, but all eyes were on Callan. That's not a fair assessment of the situation since all eyes were *usually* on Callan, even when she wasn't dressed and coifed to regal perfection as she was today. But no one doubted this was Callan's ceremony from beginning to end.

She opened with an impassioned account of what bards are already calling the Weather War, lauding the bravery and dedication of the men standing before her and acknowledging the sacrifices of those who journeyed home in coffins. Her eyes shining with unshed tears, Callan personally presented the families of those who never returned with folded Mordanian flags and a Cross of Morda, awarded only to those who give their lives in the service of their country. She referred to family members by name, hugged wives and parents, kissed children, and briefly shared grief with all of them.

She presented the same honors to the families of the *Wind Dancer's* three lost crewmen. Flown to Morda by Federation representatives, the poor people were still struggling to come to grips with their losses. At least the families of the Naval airmen recognized this day might come. Merchant airmen rarely face such dangers, leaving their families unprepared for tragic news.

With the hardest part of the ceremony out of the way, Callan recognized each of the crewmen standing before her—including the crew of the *Wind Dancer*—giving special recognition to the Marines who tossed Thor overboard and the Marine Sergeant who tackled her to the ground and shielded her with his body.

When she finished with her presentations to the surviving crewmen, everyone expected Callan to return to the dais and officially end the ceremony. Instead, she called, "Jade Cochran, please step forward."

The blonde's eyes widened and her equally surprised mother had to give her a little shove to get her moving toward Callan. The girl stopped in front of Callan and curtsied. "Yes, Your Highness?"

"Jade, you risked and almost lost your life aiding in the rescue of the surviving crew of the *Vanguard*. In light of the destruction of the mountain base, there can be no doubt that your actions saved their lives and, quite likely, the Prince Consort's life as well. We all owe you a debt beyond repayment." A servant presented an open box to Callan. She withdrew an ornate, star-shaped medal dangling from a green and gold ribbon and fastened it around Jade's neck. "From a grateful country and an equally grateful princess, please accept the Princess's Star, our highest civilian award for courage and service to the throne."

Callan kissed the girl on each cheek, lingering to whisper, "David also thanks you for pushing me from the pinnace before you went after him."

Callan was absolutely right about that. I don't know how my actions would have changed had Callan been present, but it's likely Captain Jorson and the *Tercel* would have been wrecked in the second windstorm had Callan not been there to describe the weather control device and tell him where to look for it. That, alone, probably saved dozens of lives.

Jade giggled and waited for Callan to dismiss her back to her family. Instead, Callan motioned for the girl to stay where she was.

Callan once again addressed the gathered crowd. "Ensign Christopher Marlow, please step forward."

Just as surprised as his new girlfriend, Chris managed a parade ground march to the foot of the dais. He bowed deeply and said, "I am yours to command, Your Highness."

"Rise, Ensign," Callan responded formally. "After surviving the crash of the *Vanguard* and avoiding death or capture by trogs serving our enemy, Ensign Marlow thought only of finding and aiding the Prince Consort and me. He did exactly that, providing invaluable assistance tracking the trogs to the mountain base. It was near the cave entrance that we found ourselves trapped by a large number of trogs, all armed with blaster rifles. Thinking only to protect David and me, Ensign Marlow offered up his own life to keep our presence secret. By the grace of God, the shots fired at him missed. I mourned him for dead, not knowing one of the trogs had knocked out Ensign Marlow and taken him captive.

"In the hours that followed his capture, Chris aided and protected his fellow prisoners, taking on extra duties so injured crewmen could rest and recover. During the escape orchestrated by the Prince Consort, only Chris's quick action saved Jade from tumbling to her death. While his deeds in the battle that followed were valorous and a credit to him, Ensign Marlow's ready willingness to sacrifice his own life to protect ours and Jade's are deserving of special recognition."

The same servant presented another box to Callan, from which she drew another green and gold ribbon to which an emerald-encrusted gold cross was attached. Chris's eyes widened at the sight of the medal.

"Could you bend over slightly so I can reach around your neck, Chris?" Callan asked in a low voice.

Chris did as Callan asked and she fastened the ribbon behind his neck. "From a grateful country and an equally grateful royal family, for actions above and beyond the call of duty I award you the Queen's Cross, the second highest military award for valor our country presents."

After Callan kissed Chris on both cheeks, Queen Elaina rose and kissed him on the forehead, adding her private thanks for protecting her daughter. Chris bowed low to his queen and princess. Then Callan turned Chris and Jade to face the crowd and linked arms with them.

"Ladies and gentlemen, officers and airmen, in the history of Mordan only our beloved, late Milo earned the Princess's Star at a younger age than Jade. And no member of the Mordanian Navy has earned the Queen's Cross at such a young age as Ensign Marlow." Callan paused to smile at each of them. "These two are shining examples of the kind of young people our country and our world produces. Look upon them and feel hope, for Aashla's future rests on the shoulders of such bright and brave young men and women."

Callan stepped back and gently pushed Chris and Jade together. Immediately, the crews of the *Vanguard* and the *Tercel* raised their voices, cheering loudly for the blushing teenagers. A second later, the rest of the crowd joined in and the audience chamber rang with applause.

OF COURSE YOU'RE A HERO

Chris

W hile growing up, I dreamed of the day I'd stand before the royal family and receive an award for valor from the beautiful Princess Callan. Most boys have such dreams at one time or another. Actually having that dream come true was even more exciting than I ever imagined. I just didn't expect the embarrassment I felt, too.

In your dreams, you swell with pride as your deeds are recounted before your shipmates and the nobles of the court. In your dreams, you know you deserve such praise and are worthy of the admiration directed at you. In your dreams, you're like David Rice—resolute in the face of danger, an implacable foe of evil, and certain of your rightful place in the pantheon of heroes.

Throughout the ceremony, I kept waiting for someone to point at me and shout, "Hey, he's not a hero—he's just a kid!" But no one did that. They did something worse. They cheered. For me. And for Jade, but at least *she* deserved it.

The next thing I knew my shipmates were slapping my back and pumping my hand. Then the officers saluted me—even Captain Wright—and told me I was shaping up to be a fine young officer.

When the officers and crew parted, it was to let my family

through. Mom hugged me and kissed me and cried and told me how much she loved me. Dad squeezed my shoulder and, in a voice husky with emotion, said he was so proud of me he was about to burst. The scariest part was my brothers and sisters. They were *nice* to me and said they always knew I'd make a name for myself.

Then we were whisked off to a fancy ball where lords and ladies shook my hand and told me they expected great things from me. Admirals saluted me and their wives introduced giggling daughters to me. I found every dance on my card taken up with the admirals' daughters or admirals' wives. All I really wanted to do was dance with Jade, to look into her green eyes and find a little sanity in this strange world I'd been thrust into. But Jade was busy dancing with lordlings and the sons of merchant princes.

Finally, Callan used her royal prerogative and placed herself at the top of my dance card. She whirled me out onto the dance floor, leading without appearing to lead. She studied me for a moment before asking, "What's bothering you, Chris? And don't tell me it's dancing with every eligible young lady in the court except Jade. It's something deeper than that."

I opened my mouth to respond, but the words wouldn't come. How could I tell my future ruler she'd given an award to someone who didn't deserve it? Instead, I just shook my head.

Callan gazed at me thoughtfully for a few seconds then said, "Let me guess. You think you're just a regular ensign who doesn't deserve all of this attention, much less the Queen's Cross, and you're just waiting for someone to realize it's all a mistake."

My mouth dropped open and I blurted, "How did you know?"

Callan leaned closer to me and whispered, "Because I've heard the same thing from David half a dozen times."

My mouth dropped open a second time. "David? But he's a true hero! He deserves every honor given him and more."

"If you ask David, he'll tell you he's just a man doing his duty as best he can," Callan said.

I found myself nodding vigorously. "Yes, that's exactly how I feel!"

"May I tell you a secret, Chris?" Callan asked. When I nodded, she continued, "A hero is someone who does their duty and keeps on doing their duty no matter how trying the circumstances." Callan brought us to a halt in the middle of the dance floor, took my hands in hers, and stared deeply into my eyes. "And *you*, my young Ensign, are a hero."

David and Jade spun to a stop next to us and I heard David say, "Of course he's a hero. And so is Jade!"

"But I don't feel like a hero!" Jade and I said at the same time. We looked at each other in amazement and both said, "Of course you're a hero!"

Callan deftly maneuvered Jade into my arms. "I'm declaring both of your dance cards closed except to each other for the rest of the ball. Dance or don't dance, but do so together." Callan laid a hand lightly on Jade's arm. "Oh, and Chris has been so sweet he really deserves a kiss. I thought about giving him one, but why would he want to kiss an old married woman when he can kiss the most beautiful young lady in the palace?"

"Who, me?" Jade asked in surprise.

I pulled her close and said, "Yes, you."

And, right there in the middle of the crowded dance floor, in plain sight of both of our families, the admiralty, and the gathered nobility, I kissed the most beautiful young lady in the palace and in my universe.

YOU MIGHT ALSO ENJOY...

More *Scout* adventures are coming. In the meantime, you might enjoy *The Fugitive Heir*, the first book in another series by Henry. Available now!

If you enjoyed *Scout's Law*, please post a brief review. Reader recommendations are the best advertising.

ABOUT THE AUTHOR

 Growing up, Henry worked at the usual range of menial jobs before ending up in software development. In between the menial jobs and the IT jobs, he achieved some small fame as the writer and co-creator of the small press comic book titles Southern Knights and X-Thieves. In 2006, Henry also took up the mantle of professional storyteller. He performs regularly throughout the state of North Carolina and has recently released his first book of children's stories.

Henry has been a fan of science fiction for as long as he can remember. He has loved space opera and planetary romance since the beginning, that is why his science fiction novels end up in those subgenres.

Henry currently lives in Raleigh, NC, with his wife, son, two cats, and lots of imaginary friends all clamoring to tell him of their adventures.

www.henryvogelwrites.com

ALSO BY HENRY VOGEL

Scout series

Scout's Honor

Scout's Oath

Scout's Duty

Scout's Law

Scout's Training (coming soon)

Hart for Adventure (coming soon)

The Adventures of Matt & Michelle

The Fugitive Heir

The Fugitive Pair

The Fugitive Snare

Captain Nancy Martin

The Counterfeit Captain

The Undercover Captain

The Recognition series

The Recognition Run

The Recognition Rejection

The Recognition Revelation

Other Space Opera Novels

The Lost Planet

Illustrated Children's Book

I'm in Charge! and Other Stories